PASSPORT TO YESTERDAY

# PASSPORT TO YESTERDAY

### A NOVEL IN ELEVEN STORIES

## YURI DRUZHNIKOV

Translated from the Russian by
Thomas Moore

PETER OWEN
LONDON AND CHESTER SPRINGS

PETER OWEN PUBLISHERS
73 Kenway Road, London SW5 0RE

Peter Owen books are distributed in the USA by
Dufour Editions Inc., Chester Springs, PA 19425-0007

Translated from the Russian *Viza v pozavchera*

First published in Great Britain 2004 by
Peter Owen Publishers

Original drawings by M. Belomlinsky

ISBN 0 7206 1218 7

Printed and bound in Great Britain by
MPG Books Ltd, Bodmin, Cornwall

# LILAC AND THE MAESTRO

*Cra-a-ack! Swiiiiisssshhhh!*

They were breaking off lilac sprigs in the front garden. They would bend the tips of the branches to the ground, tearing them off with a juicy crunch and then letting the branches go, and the branches, springing back, would fly upwards. Lilac fever had enveloped the whole village.

The landlady, Auntie Pasha, not yet old but having lost her feminine shape to such an extent that you couldn't even compare her to anything, oozing malice, shouted at the invisible enemy from behind her fence: 'I'll be after you with a pitchfork! And then I'm reporting you!'

The crunching subsided.

'Good grief, there's more and more of those strippers all the time!' she added, already without any spite. 'Snapping and crackling all over the place. You could go and rip off as much as your heart desires at your own place. But, no! Hell's bells, they've always got to lust after someone else's . . .'

Pasha railed on like a madwoman, promising not to sleep that night, to stand guard with a gun (that she didn't have), to catch a hooligan and take him to the district policeman to make an example of him. Even though that worthy was an alcoholic, he would be up to gaoling whoever needed it. Then the hooligan would be put away for a spell. Others were in the nick for nothing at all, but here was something for real. Pasha threatened to get an Alsatian from the NKVD kennel where her son-in-law worked.

'Tear any sod to bits,' she added, and it wasn't too clear who would do the tearing, her son-in-law or the dog.

Pasha was angry because she had been harvesting sprigs off her bushes herself. Wrapping them in a damp rag, she would take them to the town station to sell them in bouquets to greeters and seers-off. There was all the unpaid labour you could ever want on the collective farm, but there was money to be made this way. The lilac would wilt on the long road there, and Pasha would have to stand around for a long time for just a little money. Someone on holiday from the city advised her not to bring the flowers with her but to buy them at half-price from people who had been met already and resell them at full price to the next lot to arrive.

'What am I, some kind of black-marketeer?' Pasha answered indignantly and gave up the job. But letting other people steal her own lilac was something she still couldn't take.

Meanwhile, her threats hadn't frightened the strippers. Even three-year-old toddlers passing by Pasha's house would stick their hands through the cracks in the rotten fence, aiming to get hold of some flowering sprigs. *Swiiiissshhh!*

Pasha's lilac, to her misfortune, was the most beautiful in the village. The bushes shot right up over the roof of her flimsy cabin. Whenever accordion dances came to a halt around midnight on the outskirts of the village the ladies' men – off to the nearest patch of woods with their conquests in tow – would break off huge branches from Auntie Pasha's bushes on their way, and the smell of the lilac would work its magic without fail. Experts would say that there is something in its smell that does this, something to weaken basic feminine intractability. Then groans and lamentations would issue from the woods for some time, so that a stranger would surely come to the conclusion that wood-sprites were carrying on. In the words of her dead grandmother, Pasha recounted that such special lilac had been brought back by the local landowner, Colonel of Dragoons Murov, from somewhere in the Orient, where the Russian officer had been an honoured guest in the harem of some sheikh. With the help of that magical lilac the sheikh had apparently shown his guest the amorous potential of that part of the harem that served the colonel.

After coming back home, the master decided to emulate the progressive achievements of the Orient and set up premises for a harem on his estate, planting his imported special lilac saplings around it. Auntie Pasha recounted with pride how her grandmother had been quite a good-looker and had had the honour of labouring in that harem. Murov had been planning to invite the sheikh for a visit in order to prove to him that in Russia we hadn't been born yesterday and all the joys of life here were no whit worse, but then came the Revolution.

After 1917 the peasants burned down Murov's house in celebration of their new life, and Murov himself disappeared. The lilac itself ran wild on the site of the fire and spread. Pasha's son-in-law from the NKVD dog kennels said that Murov had apparently turned up somewhere, that he had written to Comrade Beria about knowing of a mighty aphrodisiac for the acquisition of female love. Murov was specially interrogated about it, agents even coming to the village for some lilac, and Beria personally conducted experiments. For a long time Murov wrote letters, but was finally advised to shut up, because Comrade Beria had said: 'There is not and can be no better aphrodisiac than the NKVD.'

'So the lilac became the people's, that is, mine, now,' as Auntie Pasha explained Bolshevik party policy. 'Mine! And the whole district is hankering after it. Have a sniff, and after you sniff your fill, take off to the woods to do your screwing. That wouldn't hurt a thing, but those sods . . .'

It was a good thing they hadn't let the colonel out, Auntie Pasha thought. Pasha's old man had put together this lop-sided cabin from the unburnt timbers of the Murov house. If the master were to come back he would demand the return of his wood. For the last three summers Pasha had been renting out a part of the cabin to a family of vacationers named Nemets. Papa was a Nemets, Mama was a Nemets, their son was a Nemets, and their daughter was a Nemets, too – something that sounds like 'German' in Russian. Of course, they were Russians. Their grandfather was from the Tambov village of Nemtsy, in whose name the stress falls on the last syllable. But judge for yourselves, comrade sirs: who beyond the bounds of that village would pronounce the word *nemets* with the accent shifted to the end? So they just had to put up with it. But when that's the case, who's going to consider someone a Russian, a Tatar or an Aleut if their name means 'German'? And if you aren't, after all, some kind of German with a name like that, then what are you?

*Ssswiiisshhhhhh!*

At first light, Oleg would be instantly awake at the crunching sound of a branch hitting the house wall and snapping back into position. Oleg slept behind that very wall. He would start up in fright and peer out of the window but wouldn't be able to see anything in the gloom. The lilac wouldn't let light through even in the daytime. Outside, women's squeals and whispers could be heard.

Oleg's mother woke up as well at the crackling on this particular morning and said to his father, 'That lilac won't last till Sunday, oh, no, it won't . . . !'

It hadn't been a month since the Nemetses had moved into the *dacha*. Father would spend weeknights in the city. From the village to the station was a one-hour walk over the fields and another hour's travel on the train, and in the city it was a little way further still, on the tram from the terminal, and in the case of a power failure, when the tram wouldn't operate, yet another hour's walk on foot. He would arrive back on Saturday evening. On those days Mother would let Oleg off practising his violin later in the day, and that was wonderful. He and Lyuska would go to meet their father at the edge of the village, taking turns to rock in the iron seat of the collective farm's rusting haymow, half sunk into the ground. Pasha assured everyone that the mower had been solemnly presented to the collective by a representative of the Bolshevik Party on the orders of Lenin himself.

'But no one can quite recollect his name,' Pasha said to Oleg's father. 'Either it was Dear-Jinsky, or it was Mine-Jinsky, but anyhow it must've been Lunar-Charsky. In a word, out of the NKVD, from Lenin.'

'Lenin had already died before there were any collective farms, though,' his father said in surprise, but Pasha knew her history better.

'Died or didn't die, it was him who told them to give us the mower. That's the reason the chairman hangs on to it, and we just mow by hand now.'

Oleg's father preferred not to get any deeper into a political discussion. Even by hand, there was very little mowing being done on the collective farm's fields; everyone was working at their own plots of land, for their own sustenance, although for not showing up in the fields the chairman threatened to cut off 'Ilyich's lightbulb' – the supply of electricity to their houses. But the mower, although rusted, had become an element of culture, so to speak. At night during the dances the accordion player would settle himself on its iron bucket seat, and the haymow would find itself at the centre of a dance floor of well-trampled grass.

Coming back from the city, their father would usually come into sight on the path that zigzagged out of the ravine and went through the meadow spotted with cowpats and some cornflower-shot rough grass that wasn't attractive even to Pasha's ageing goat, Zorka. Pasha would try to stake Zorka out somewhere in sight, so that the goat could lower itself down into the ravine on the rope for juicier grass. But Zorka didn't have the slightest inclination to be a mountain goat; she didn't like climbing, and her dissatisfied bleating sounded like whining.

On the lookout for his father, Oleg would run down to the marsh and bring back grass and fresh shoots for the goat. Lyuska would feed her by hand, while Oleg would draw circles and figures of eight around them on his bicycle. Zorka would keep silent while dealing with the food but would then again begin to whimper, almost like a dog. It was impossible either to feed her up or cheer her up. Lyuska and Oleg were upset by Zorka's plight but would instantly forget about the goat as soon as they caught sight of their father across the ravine. They would rush to meet him: Lyuska running, Oleg pedalling with all his might.

'Easy, take it easy,' their father would yell at Oleg from below, puffing up the path from the ravine. 'You'll crash, you mad nutter!'

'Can there be an unmad nutter?' Oleg would ask, reaching his father and starting to ride in circles around him.

'Sure there can,' his father would retort. 'Lyuska over here – she's an unmad nutter, but you . . . ?'

This time he was walking heavily laden as well: he had been paid, and the next day was a holiday. A real *dacha*-bound husband, he was carrying two huge bags and – Oleg noticed this right away – a real bamboo fishing rod. He hadn't forgotten but had remembered his promise. For sure, now, they would be going fishing when his father's own vacation began. And presents for everyone – for Oleg, for Lyuska and for their mother – were sticking out of the bags.

His parents' fifteenth wedding anniversary was on Wednesday. And his father and mother had suddenly started bustling around, getting things ready, storing up groceries, even though they had never celebrated their anniversary before. They had decided to have the party on Sunday. Their guests could arrive during the day, go swimming in the stream, walk in the woods and generally take a break from the city's hubbub and stuffy heat.

'The table won't be that full, but lilac – you'll be able to breathe in lilac to your heart's content,' promised their father, inviting his relatives and friends. 'And you can take some home with you. Our landlady has lilac, the best lilac in the whole village. If you don't believe me, come and see for yourself!'

Lively Lyuska turned out to be the more agile and reached her father first today. She stopped, waiting for a hug from her father. He couldn't manage it because of the bags. Oleg rode up, pedalling furiously. Their father put his bags and his briefcase on the grass, set down the fishing rod and hugged the children both at once.

'Seems to me you've grown in the last week,' he said to Lyuska. 'You'll be taller than me soon, eh?'

Lyuska only snorted. She was simply aching to grow up so that she could go to the dances at the haymow, but she hadn't managed it yet. She was thirteen, but still nobody thought her grown up. She was beginning to catch the eye of passers-by, though, and she was able to figure out something of what that meant, but who knew what that was.

'Well, my birthday strollers, how're things? Is your mother cooking? Have you been waiting for me? Right you are!'

It was very nice for Oleg and Lyuska that the Nemetses' family custom was to make all family holidays into birthday parties for the children. Their father bent over and rooted around in a bag, took out a box and handed it over to his daughter. She took it without a word and went off to one side. And suddenly her cheeks flushed deep red: she took out a new pair of brown high-heeled shoes.

'And me?' Oleg asked politely. He had noticed his present long before but was waiting for it.

'This is for you.' His father indicated the collapsible fishing rod. 'And something else . . .'

Oleg threw down his bike and grabbed the rod. And when he turned around, his father handed him a package. Oleg tore it open on the spot. In it was a selection of floats, hooks and metal lures.

'Wo-o-ow!' Oleg yelled, loud enough that Zorka jumped to one side and bleated. Her bleating done with, she stared with frightened eyes at the people. Lyuska sat down on the grass, took her new, brown, high-heeled shoes back out of their box and put them straight away on her dirty bare feet. Then she strolled back and forth in the heels in front of her father.

'Look at you flouncing! You're a girl from a proper family. Ask your mum how to swing your . . .'

He didn't finish saying what.

Oleg was counting his hooks and lures.

'An' me-e-e-e?' Zorka said, putting off chewing her grass.

Nobody paid her any attention. Oleg, getting back on his bike, rode on ahead, holding his rod in one hand. His lengthening shadow ran along in front of him. It was hopping from mound to mound, jerking back and forth as if trying to tear itself away from the bicycle and hurtle off into the distance.

His sister took off her high heels so as not to get them dirty, wiped the dust off them with her hand and ambled along barefoot behind them, not taking her eyes off the shoes. She was thinking over how to put them on that night without her mother finding out.

But her mother was already running towards them. The open gate, the lilac bushes in the front garden, the earthenware pots drying on the fence posts, and their mother's face, happy and excited – everything was crimson in the beams of the lowering sun. The sun was hanging right above the ravine, heavy, ready to press down, to crush the meadow, the village, the lilac bushes, all the people, and even the goat Zorka beneath it. Never had Oleg seen such a heavy sunset, neither before this nor later, after he had grown up and seen everything.

While his mother was bustling over supper, his father unhurriedly set up the samovar in the yard alongside the porch. The side of the samovar was burning in the sun, as if it were about to melt. Oleg zipped around his father on his bike.

'Don't bother your father, Olya!' his mother yelled from the porch.

'He's not Olya, he's Oleg! Didn't we agree on that?' contradicted his father, coughing in the smoke. 'Anyway, we should have called him Franz, in honour of Schubert.'

'That would be the last straw! They'd never stop teasing him, then. It's bad enough that his name sounds like "German".'

'But you wouldn't call him Olya, then, would you!'

Father didn't like it when Mother called the boy by a woman's name. But she was accustomed to it.

It was getting dark. Oleg didn't want to get off his bicycle, even when everyone else had taken their seats at the table on the porch.

What was the rush, if his mother was only going to send him to bed right after supper? But his father got up and led him to the table by the hand.

They were sitting in the twilight without turning on their lights, so as not to attract any mosquitoes. Their father was joking, laughing, trying to cheer up their mother, who was exhausted by her long day. A whitish fog was rising out of the ravine and creeping along the ground. It enveloped the veranda and wanted to come right up on to it but evidently wouldn't take the risk. It was getting chilly. A butterfly flew up to the warmth and settled on the samovar. But it couldn't hang on; its legs crumpled and it fell down the chimney, on to the burnt-out coals.

'How's the fiddler doing?' their father said, suddenly stern.

'You know, he's become awfully lazy.' His mother looked at Oleg. 'Instead of four hours, he plays two at the most. You'd have to tie him up with a rope.'

Oleg decided to keep quiet in order not to make things worse. The autumn before last they had started him in music school, and his teacher had told him to practise every day in summer as well. It was hard enough for adults to endure forced labour, but Oleg really suffered from it.

'You'll pedal your talents away,' grumbled his mother, 'and you a boy from a good family.'

'That's all right. Tomorrow's a holiday for us,' said the senior Nemets. 'But from this Monday on our son will start playing for real. Isn't that right? It's always better to start on Monday.'

The logic was doubtful, but right now it was to Oleg's advantage, and he willingly agreed to it. The whole of Sunday lay ahead of him before it was Monday.

'Hurry up with your food!' his mother urged him. 'You're up past your bedtime already. And we have to get up early: we've got guests coming.'

She was longing for her husband. But Oleg had missed him, too, and didn't want to go to bed. Only Lyuska surreptitiously threw her gaze to the bench where the shoes lay, and thoughts were jostling one another in her little head, twined all over in black curls that she would now and again wind around a finger. Was it the smell from the lilac that was disturbing her? On the other side of the wall the landlady, Auntie Pasha, sighed heavily, turning over on her trestle bed. In the barn not far from the cabin Zorka complained offendedly.

'Me-e-e-e-e!' she kept repeating despondently.

From all of these: from the darkness, the rank smoke from the samovar, the thick smell of the lilac, from the fog that enveloped the garden, the mosquitoes' grating whine and their father's laughter – from all of these came some kind of mysteriousness that caught at the breath. It seemed to Oleg that this evening would never become night, and he didn't feel like interrupting it, leaving, going to bed.

'Sleep, go to sleep, it's bedtime,' his mother nagged.

If only she had known that today was the last day of childhood for Lyuska and Oleg, that now they would be saying farewell to it. If she *had* known she might have allowed them to stay up at least another half an hour.

An accordion began to play in the street. Somebody was clapping in time with it, whooping and dancing. Lyuska went into their room and stole up to the window. Her mother didn't like her to do that. Lyuska had just yesterday run off to the haymow to watch the dancing, and her mother had had to go to fetch her, threatening to drag her home.

Their mother exchanged glances with their father, took Oleg by the hand and, without listening to his objections, took him off to bed. Their father went over to Lyuska. He got along with her better. He hugged her around the shoulders from the side, trying not to touch her feminine charms, which had become quite protuberant that summer. He said that she didn't have much growing left to do – something like three years, and then she could dance all day long and all her life long. Lyuska sighed.

'You don't understand anything! In three years I'll be an old maid. Who's going to choose me then?'

She offendedly shrugged her shoulder and went off to bed to listen to the couples by the lilac bushes whispering to one another.

Oleg tossed and turned for a long while, looking at his fishing rod standing in the corner, and had already fallen asleep when the familiar '*Cra-ack! Ssswii-ii-iisshhhh!*' resounded from behind the wall, over his head. The village lads were giving Auntie Pasha's lilac to their girl-friends before strolling off into the dark woods. Oleg fell asleep to the music.

In the morning Nemets junior awoke to the twittering of birds. The first thing he saw was his child-sized violin hanging on its nail above his bed. Over by the opposite wall Lyuska was still sleeping sweetly. Behind the window, starlings were trying to find a more comfortable perch in the shade of the lilac and argumentatively discussed their vital concerns. The sun was rising quickly. His mother was clattering dishes in her hurry and making her magic over the kerosene stove, on which stood a sooty baking-oven. The stove was smoking, but two browned pastry rings were sitting pretty on the table already, with a third baking away.

'What do you think, how many people are coming?' their mother asked their father for the umpteenth time. 'How many of yours and how many of mine?'

'Yours' meant the father's relatives, 'mine' the mother's.

'About twenty people, if not more – the whole International,' he answered, 'and the four of us and the representative of the common people.'

Auntie Pasha, the representative of the common people, had brought over dishes, knives, forks, and his mother told Oleg to set them around the table on the porch. Oleg counted out loud.

'But anyway,' his father observed, 'you'd better go and practise for an hour while nobody's here. You have to warm up your fingers every day!'

'You said yourself – starting this Monday!' objected Oleg.

And his father had nothing to top that with. He took the bag with its bottles of vodka and wine out to the cold-store and decided to chop up some dry pine kindling for the samovar in advance. He handled the hatchet with dexterity, and the pile of kindling grew quickly.

After milking Zorka, Auntie Pasha brought over the earthenware pot full of milk, slung her yoke over her shoulder, snatched up the buckets and set off for the well. Oleg jumped his bicycle off the porch and followed along after her. The well was next to the neighbouring cabin. The windows of that cabin were wide open, and the breeze was blowing the curtains out through them. They looked like sails. Oleg started riding in circles around the well, raising dust, until Auntie Pasha chased him away. She filled one bucket, then lowered the second down and started to raise it. The winch groaned. Pasha scooped up some water from the bucket in her palm and poured it on the axle so that it wouldn't squeak.

In the cabin someone turned the radio up. Coming to life in mid-word, it screamed; it wasn't clear what it was about. Auntie Pasha turned her head and listened. Oleg listened to it, too, but didn't understand anything and rode off around the well again. Here he saw that Auntie Pasha had let go of the winch handle. The bucket, full of water, crashed off the log framework of the well with a roar, plunging madly to the bottom. Forgetting her full pail and the yoke on the grass, Auntie Pasha ran to her home. Her scarf came undone, her hair tumbling free over her shoulders. Without understanding what had happened, Oleg raced off after her.

Pasha came to a halt, flinging open the gate. The burdocks disturbed by the gate waved their enormous leaves in surprise. Gulping air, Pasha stared from the children's mother, busy at the kerosene stove with the bake-oven, to their father, kneeling and wielding the hatchet to chop the kindling. The gate swung back, squeaking, and Oleg's mother turned her head.

'What's up, Auntie Pasha? Is that our guests showing up already?'

It was as if Pasha had lost her tongue.

'What's up with you?' his mother asked again, in alarm. 'You've gone white as a sheet . . .'

'Wa . . .' Pasha breathed out, her eyes darting, her throat constricted. She was groaning, ready to fall over, it looked like, but then she gathered herself up. 'Wa . . . r,' she finally managed to say.

'War games, must be,' the father said, without turning his head. 'And you're scared? That's a laugh.'

He kept on splitting chunks of the wood with his hatchet. But not as confidently as before.

'But it's war, ah . . . It's the war!' Auntie Pasha repeated, losing control of herself. 'War, for sure, folks. Oy . . . !'

'Mummy!' squealed Lyuska and threw herself on her mother's neck.

Her father got up off the grass, throwing away the hatchet. The smile slowly slid from his face. He turned pale.

'Who says?'

'The radio, who else could say something like that?' Auntie Pasha's sense and voice had suddenly come back to her.

'So who's the war with, then?' Father asked incredulously.

Auntie Pasha, suddenly seeing the light, stared at him.

'What do you mean, with who? With you, with the Germans!'

'How can you talk like that, Auntie Pasha?' he said indignantly.

''Tisn't me! It's that Mollytov who just announced it: the Germans have attacked. He says that we got to save Comrade Stalin, or he'll be the first to get it. And if he gets it, who's going to protect us?'

A woman started howling in the neighbouring house, then another one; children started screaming, dogs barking.

'Then what the hell are we standing here for?' asked the father. 'We have to . . .'

He fell silent. Oleg was surprised that even his father didn't know what to do if war came. His father stared intently into the sky, as if making an effort to read something very important up there. As if it were written there that he had two months and four days left until his dying breath. And his mother with as much time until she became a widow.

They got ready to leave the *dacha*, spasmodically, absurdly. Their father took the bundles of groceries out of his bag and put them on the table. Their mother, clenching her teeth, put their belongings into the bag and their two suitcases.

Their father took down the violin from its nail and held it out to Oleg: 'Take this, maestro!'

'There's why your guests didn't come!' Auntie Pasha decided. 'Now they'll be a-bombing! You're here, and over there they'll be a-bombing your property! Poor old property!'

Lyuska was standing on the steps, clutching her new shoes to her chest. Oleg didn't want to say goodbye to his new fishing rod and bicycle.

'Maybe we should leave the violin and take my bike?' he offered, carefully.

But his father decided that they would have to leave the bicycle for a while, not for long, of course, but not the violin. War or no war, he would need to practise. Sighing, Oleg gave in. He didn't know if he should be happy or upset. The grief of the adults had not spread to him, and the sudden departure seemed a fortuitous and fascinating adventure.

While they were finishing getting their things together, Pasha ran to the well to get her bucket and yoke. The second bucket had torn off the chain and sunk. Oleg's mother cut up the hot pie and gave everyone a piece.

'But me-e-e-e?' cried Zorka, who hadn't yet been taken out to pasture.

Pasha led Zorka out of the barn and tied her up in the yard next to the potato patch.

'It don't matter now,' she lamented. 'Let her eat the tops off, let everything go to blue blazes.'

The Nemetses silently carried their suitcases to the gate. The custom was to sit down together to mark the start of a journey, and they did.

Without addressing anyone in particular, suddenly Mother said: 'Shouldn't have, oh, we shouldn't have put it off till Sunday! Now when will we get the chance?'

'Hang on, it'll all get sorted out,' their father reassured her. 'Our boys will thrash them, quick as a flash. On their territory. They won't even have time to let out a squeak.'

He had wanted to say 'the Germans' but said 'they' instead.

'Hah!' their mother pronounced. 'They've been getting ready.'

'And us? Stalin hasn't been sleeping either. They said recently on the radio that he never sleeps. It's only a pity that I probably won't get my holidays now. And when everything's over, then I'll take my holidays for sure, we'll come back here again and go fishing with Oleg. Isn't that right, Auntie Pasha?'

'Maybe so,' she responded unwillingly. 'My lad never come back from the Finns, but nowadays maybe it'll be so. Who knows how things'll turn out. We got progress nowadays, they do write in the papers how we got progress now . . . Wait a bit while I break you off a bunch of lilac for the road. I'll be back in a flash, a flash . . .'

She bent down the tallest lilac bush until its old trunk cracked, and began mercilessly tearing off huge sprigs with their bright violet-coloured flowers. The Nemetses put their things on the ground again and stood at a loss, waiting. The sun was high, and the lilac bunches were wilting and shrinking in the heat.

'The five-petalled ones didn't do us any good,' their mother suddenly said.

Every day Oleg and Lyuska had climbed amongst the branches looking for the rare blossoms with five petals. They had found lots of the starry flowers. Whenever she found one, Lyuska would giggle, but why, Oleg didn't understand. She would hold the flower between her palms and whisper something. Oleg would take the five-petalled flower to his mother. She would always be glad and would say: 'This one's for luck! And this one . . .'

'Take it, go on, why not . . . ?' mumbled Pasha, heaping the great huge bouquet on to their mother. 'It don't matter – the lilac's all going to die now anyhow. They'll take the lads away into the army now, and who'll be breaking sprigs off for the girls from such a height? And lilac'll wither away if you don't break some off. Like a woman with her flower ungot. You have to take the flowers off lilac-bushes and women when they be blooming. 'Cause with their flowers ungot they'll wither away. They be longing for someone's hands to get them!'

'How come you wouldn't let them pluck any, then?' their mother asked without any curiosity.

'Oh, my dear hearts,' Pasha flung up her hands. 'Wouldn't let them? I was just angry 'cause they were squeezing each other and here I am, all on my own. And besides . . . When was it, anyway? That was before the war. But nowadays . . . And what's going to happen to you folks? You be Germans, after all, that is to say, our enemies, nowadays . . .'

'But that's just a family name!'

'Oooooh, that's even worse! Everybody'll see it, clear as a sore on your nose! And then what'll happen! Here you are, take it!'

Pasha heaped a second huge bouquet into Oleg's arms. He clutched one arm around the lilac in perplexity and with the other pressed the towel-wrapped violin to his stomach. In single file they plodded off down the path leading to the station.

After several steps Oleg turned around. Pasha was standing with her back to him and was breaking branches off furiously, one after another.

*Cra-a-ack! Snap! Swi-i-i-shhh!*

She threw them maniacally to the ground, trampling them under her feet, uttering words that Oleg had scarcely heard before, and later on, after he had become a man, tried never to use in front of women.

# SOLOIST WITHOUT A FIDDLE

Before dressing Oleg in his navy-blue sailor's jumper with its white appliqué sail on the front, his mother spent a long time scrubbing him all over with a facecloth and then clipped his fingernails and toenails.

'Why my toenails?' he asked. 'Nobody's going to see them.'

'Just in case,' she explained.

His mother proceeded to feel over his hands, as if he had nine fingers or had just fallen down on some gravel and scraped his palms bloody. But everything was sound as a bell. Meanwhile, Lyuska was snickering. She didn't believe in human talent at all, neither her own nor others'.

His parents were dressing up as if for the theatre. His father decked himself out in his Sunday-best blue suit and put on his dark-red tie with diagonal blue-and-white stripes, which was clearly strangling him. His mother put on her black dress with the lace collar (Oleg and his father both liked it on her) and her only pair of smart shoes with high, high heels. Finally they made him blow his nose twice into his father's handkerchief, so as not to mess up his own, then led him off. Lyuska stayed at home, sprawled on the couch with a book. She hadn't even asked her mother to let her try on the high-heeled shoes, which she had usually done before.

This took place two years before the war. The semi-dark corridor of the two-storeyed mansion on Tatarskaya Street was jam-packed with children and even more parents, gathered together in nervous anticipation of the interviews to come. Some of them were reading the announcement on the wall: 'Children over five years of age according to their birth certificate are not accepted into the first violin class.' This didn't concern Oleg, but other visitors shook their heads, muttered something and took their children away, empty-handed. Without anything to do, the Nemets father and son started playing slap-my-hand.

'Have you lost your minds?' his mother whispered, looking angrily at his father. 'Stop that this minute! You're going to knock the fingers off the boy right before his interview.'

'Is there a Nemets here?' asked a stern, grey-haired woman with a white bow under her chin, opening the door a crack.

Everyone started looking around for a foreigner.

'Here, of course we are!' his father reacted.

'Birth certificate, please.'

She passed her eyes over the document, checking the date of birth, and turned away, motioning them to follow her. Oleg's father pushed him towards the door but stayed behind himself, taking Oleg's mother by the hand. Oleg took several steps and, his mouth open, stopped at the threshold at a loss.

The woman with the white bow sat at a grand piano. A dazzling antique silver brooch gleamed on her blouse. 'Hello, my little friend. So, your surname is Nemets and your first name is Oleg, is that so?'

Oleg nodded obediently.

'Do you like to sing?'

Oleg nodded again. He was interestedly scrutinizing the brooch on the woman's bosom – he had never seen anything like it in his life. She beckoned him towards her, took his little hands into hers and began turning them over, squeezing and measuring them against her own. Then she wrote down something in her notebook.

'So, you like to sing? Then sing me a song that you like.'

Oleg knew all the songs that were current before the war.

'*There are lots of grand girls in the collective, but you're only going to fall in love with one!*' he started bawling.

He was trying very hard; his father had told him to sing as loud as he could, but the woman narrowed her eyes and waved her hand at him.

'Enough, enough, darling! That's plenty! Now I'll play and you'll beat out the rhythm on the piano top with your hand. Understood?'

What was there not to understand?

She placed one hand on the keyboard and played a short melody. Figuring it out was easy as pie: '*Wide is my native land*'. Oleg drummed along. The woman nodded and wrote down something on the slip of paper. The brooch on her bosom jiggled.

'That's it!' she said dryly. 'You can go home.'

And Oleg found himself in his mother's embrace.

'You didn't forget to say goodbye, did you?'

He had to go back. Oleg opened the door once again and beheld a boy just like him, sitting there in the same sailor's jumper with his fingers getting squeezed the same way.

'Goodbye!' Oleg shouted, and slammed the door.

Several days later his father burst into their tiny room with a mysterious bundle.

'Here you go, take it! But don't drop it.'

The bundle was solemnly unwrapped. It turned out that it held a violin – a new one, smelling of wood and varnish. It hadn't been an easy thing to purchase. Oleg needed a quarter-size, the smallest violin possible. Besides the violin, the paper held a bow, a little tin of rosin and a plastic chin-rest, everything that a real violinist needed.

His father and mother exchanged glances while they watched Oleg try the violin under his chin. Happiness streamed out of his parents' eyes. In bed just before falling asleep they dreamed aloud to each other. They could see placards going up all over the city the next day: winner of all the competitions, the famous violinist Oleg Nemets will be performing, etc., etc. And here they modestly sit in the front row while their son stands at centre stage. The hall, enraptured, falls silent, and the violin in their son's hands comes to life. Now he finishes – and the audience erupts in ovation. And bouquets of flowers fly over their heads on to the stage, and so on and so forth.

Only one thing worried his parents: how were they to behave, themselves? His mother considered that they should applaud along with the rest of the audience despite the fact that it was their own son, but his father was positive that it would be better to sit modestly, eyes downcast, pretending that they had nothing to do with it. All well-bred people behaved like that. But, when they were asked to come to the stage they would modestly step out and take their bows as well.

The Nemetses were lucky. The teacher at the music school, that same stout, grey-haired woman with the white bow and brooch, turned out to be the third violin of the Opera Theatre orchestra and a great enthusiast for searching out gifted children. Her husband was first violin in the same orchestra, and her son was a newly fashionable up-and-coming young conductor whose name, if he were to come to town from the capital, would be looked for immediately on street billboards by the Nemetses. Oleg's teacher fussed again and again over her pupils, asked the parents again and again to bring the children to study with her at her home. The Nemetses took their son across the entire city again and again on clunky old buses so that Oleg could draw his bow back and forth in front of the teacher for half an hour.

Years later, sitting in an orchestra, Oleg Nemets more than once wondered why his father and mother wanted, with such passion, to make a Paganini out of their son. Why not a Rembrandt or a Newton or a Lermontov? Although Lermontov was a bad example: in childhood he, too, was taught to play – on the violin, in fact. Anyway, it would have been understandable if his parents themselves had been musicians. In that case, it would have been a matter of heredity, but here . . . ? The persistence with which his parents pursued it was and remained enigmatic, a mystery.

Right after the examination, whenever a friend rang up on the telephone his mother would inform them before anything else: 'Our Oleg was accepted into the music school! Of course, they examined him and found out how talented he is. His fingers are perfect for the violin. He has a sense of rhythm and *perr-ffect* pitch as well! He passed his exam brilliantly, that's a fact. Now everything depends entirely on his own industry.'

And Oleg's mother would turn a searching look on him.

Oleg himself, although he was happy, did not rejoice. At first it had been interesting to go to the music school accompanied by his mother and draw his bow across the strings there and guess from where the sounds were flying out. But he liked carrying the violin around on the street even more. Some passers-by would glance at you: the neck was sticking out of your newspaper. Oleg wrapped it this way on purpose so that the violin would be visible.

There were no small violin cases for sale. His mother's relative, Aunt Polina, came to his rescue. Her husband nosed the grindstone at the Khimik factory, and he smuggled out a piece of silvery material that looked like the oilcloth they made barrage balloons out of. His mother sewed a bag to fit his violin out of this material. Now whenever Oleg went to the music school absolutely everybody would stare at his silver cover.

Soon, however, Nemets junior stopped sharing his parents' raptures. He got sick and tired of playing the same old scales every day for a long time, over and over. He would rather have lain around in bed in the mornings and then played with his toys, but as soon as he got up his mother would hurry up and remind him: 'Have you forgotten about your scales? And the crossover from one string to another, like your teacher told you? You have to play a whole half hour!'

He would obediently start playing, and right away she would start in: 'You're holding the violin the wrong way! Look at the picture in the book: the wrist isn't curved this way when you draw the bow!'

His mother would speak with authority, as if the only thing she had done all her life was teach children to play the violin. Oleg would play hastily and rest at the long pauses, looking at the mockingly slow-moving hands of the clock. But the minute hand wasn't being forced to play the violin, and it wouldn't hurry around the half of the clock-face.

Even playing in the yard was less fun now than it had been before. You would scarcely get out the door and you would be expecting to be called home on the spot. And you couldn't get into a proper fight because immediately there would be a shout from the window: 'Your fingers! You'll hurt your fingers!'

Oleg grew sad: everyone else was going about their business, but . . . him? He would have been better off learning how to box. It was clear to everyone in the courtyard that it would come in a lot handier than playing the violin.

'Well, how's our maestro?' his father would ask in the meantime, coming home in the evening. And seeing his son's sour physiognomy he would add sometimes, turning to Oleg's mother: 'Listen, if the child doesn't want to do it, maybe we shouldn't torture him.'

'What!?' his mother would say indignantly. 'How would he know if he wanted to or not? He'll quit now, and then later on he'll want to, and it'll be too late.'

Over dinner his mother told his father edifying stories about famous violinists.

'Take Oistrakh, for instance . . . And that other fellow, what's his name, I've forgotten exactly, I think, Busya Goldshteyn – they had to drag him out from under his bed by force. They would beat him with a belt to make him play. And the result: the whole world knows who he is!' Then Oleg's mother would turn to him.

'And nobody beats you, Olya. They think that you understand yourself how important it is. So you just have to play of your own free will!'

Oleg's father would laugh, but he showed a united front with his wife, anyway. They would consistently fail to understand how boring and repugnant it was to stand beside the table three times a day for half an hour at a time and draw, draw, draw the bow back and forth, back and forth, back and forth . . .

The first concert given by Oleg Nemets, the violinist, wasn't in the music school but in a bomb shelter two years later. The city hadn't been bombed yet, but the air-raid sirens had started giving the alarm.

Hearing the wail of the siren, Oleg's mother had dressed him hurriedly, grabbed Lyuska with her other hand and dragged the children to the basement of a neighbouring large building. They descended the dark stairs for a long time. In the stuffy room with its blue bulb somewhere overhead, the air-duct fan whirred. All around people stood or sat, coughing, snorting, chewing, babies crying. The air-raid siren continued to wail somewhere up above.

'Play!' Oleg's mother said to him as soon as she had recovered her breath. 'It's time for you to play!'

Of course she hadn't forgotten to snatch up the violin on the way out.

Oleg felt awkward, but he obediently drew the instrument out of its silver cover, rubbed the rosin on his bow, looked around and began tuning the strings. Everyone around stopped fussing and talking. Even the babies' crying died down. Heads turned towards him.

The young Paganini started to play his exercises, crossing over from string to string, getting mixed up and starting again. The people looked at him and listened to him as if they had really found themselves all of a sudden at some violinist's concert. An intellectual-looking elderly woman, almost hairless and wrapped in a shawl, sat down next to them on the floor and swayed in rhythm to the music. Oleg went from the exercises to a simple little melody that he could already play, although not confidently.

'Quiet, citizens, don't shove! There's a musician here.'

Some of the surrounding people had begun to push their way closer, sitting down on the floor. One old man next to them grumbled: 'They've found a great place for music . . .'

They shushed the old man. It was as if people were forgetting that somewhere upstairs bombs could be dropping – or wanted to forget it. And as soon as Oleg finished and lowered his violin there came a weak applause. It seemed like a real ovation to his mother when she told his father that evening all about the concert in the bomb shelter. Oleg's father patted him on the cheek. Somewhere on the outskirts of the city the first bombs had dropped that day.

The evacuation of mothers and children began. From a tobacco stand, his father got a wooden box that had held Belomorkanal cigarettes, and they spent half an hour filling it with their belongings.

'Are we going to take my violin?' Oleg asked suddenly. 'I'll play it in the bomb shelters there. I had fun.'

His father and mother exchanged glances.

'Definitely,' his father nodded. 'Otherwise, how will you face your teacher again? You'll forget everything . . .'

At the station a crowd was buzzing around the recently arrived train. His father tried to embrace his mother, but they were being shoved from all sides.

'Hey, you've found a great place for making love!'

'Let the children through to the carriage!'

'You've certainly got yourself a lot of things!' the arm-banded marshals on the platform shouted. 'Get rid of them: we can't even squeeze people in!'

'Papers,' the female conductor demanded.

Next to her stood a man in civilian clothes. Their mother handed over her passport. The man glanced at the photograph and at Oleg's mother's face.

'Nemets – German, right,' he said, looking them over with a certain irony, 'and you're escaping from the Germans. You could stay behind . . .'

'What for?' his mother asked in alarm, sensing a trick.

'To wait for them . . .'

'But we're Russians. What are you on about?' Her voice shook. 'That's just a surname.'

'And are the children registered on your passport?'

'Yes, of course they are. Why shouldn't they be?'

'Do you have an evac notice?'

'Evac what?' His mother didn't understand.

'A document for evacuation.'

'There's the notice there, inserted in the passport.'

'Right . . . Let them into the car.'

His mother leaned out of the carriage window, and his father carefully handed over the violin to her.

'Make sure our son plays every day. It's very important, important for his future.'

'All right, all right, don't worry. Look after yourself,' answered Oleg's mother, biting her lip to keep from bursting into tears. It was as if she could sense that this was the last time they would see each other in this life.

'Look at the huge violin cover!' shouted Oleg, pointing his finger at the window.

Above the station in the fading sunlit sky hung a plump barrage balloon of the same silvery material that Polina's husband had brought home from the factory for Oleg's violin cover.

With a jerk the train started off. Oleg, his mother and Lyuska, swaying, stuck their heads through the crack in the window and, swallowing the sooty smoke from the engine, tried to look back. Pushing people away, their father ran after the railway carriage, but the platform was too crowded. Others were trying to run as well and were knocking each other down, jamming the platform. His father's face got mixed up with the others, and he disappeared. He stayed that way for ever for Oleg Nemets: dear, smiling in dismay, very distant and indistinct, looking like all the other fathers in the crowd.

The train whistled, picking up speed, and the platform with his father was left in the distance. The train was a mixed one of freight and passenger cars. A shelf to hold three people in luxury fell to the Nemetses' lot. Their mother decided that she would put the children head to toe and she would squeeze herself into a corner and sleep sitting up.

Oleg, afraid of forgetting his father's instruction, suddenly spoke up: 'I'll play for a bit, Mum! I've already missed one practice today . . .'

33

Amazed, his mother pulled the violin out of its silvery cover. The carriage was rocking. Drawing his bow back, Oleg's hand would hit against the shelf, and the sounds would come out either staccato and quavery or plaintive and doleful. The jaws of the people sitting on the neighbouring shelves dropped and their eyes followed the bow. An audience from the whole carriage, even more people than had been in the bomb shelter, gathered in the aisle.

They travelled slowly, not to any timetable, the train standing on sidings for hours at a time. At large stations his mother would dash off for the boiled water and bread that they passed out in exchange for vouchers. The carriages were now and again switched from track to track, and once his mother would have been stranded at an unknown station if a bombardment hadn't started at that very moment: the train was halted, and she managed to catch up with it. She noticed with surprise that on their trip he played his exercises three times a day and that she didn't have to make him do it. He just played. He liked it when an audience gathered in the passageway to listen to him even though he was playing the same scales over and over. But there were discontented and grumbling passengers in the carriage, too.

'You've all gone completely crazy!' a lame middle-aged woman who was looking for sympathy would say to all the passers-by, knocking her stick on the floor. 'The toilet's blocked up, and they play the fiddle . . .'

Nobody knew where they had been heading for six days and nights. At a small town near the Urals the train was driven on to a siding, and it was announced that they wouldn't be going any further.

Sighing old women in black gathered in bunches at the station to gawk at the evacuees or, as they said, *vykovyrennye*, 'the plucked-out ones' – and really that word was more precise than the strange and incomprehensible *evakuirovannye*, 'the evacuated ones'. Deputies with red armbands on their sleeves ran around with lists, distributing the people by street and house. This was called 'consolidation'. Angry householders took the people in to live with them unwillingly. But

Russians are inured to force: they give in to pressure from above without any particular resistance. The people obeyed reluctantly, but then later warmed to their guests, one lending out a kerosene stove and another some potatoes, yet another a spare pillow.

The Nemetses were set up in a rather clean room with a window facing the vegetable garden. Beyond a partition lived their host's family – he was a driver for the local meat-processing administration. Of course, there wasn't a trace of meat in the town, but there was an administrative apparatus. At first his mother suffered from the fact that the bed behind the partition would squeak at night, and then the driver's wife would get up and there would be the sound of running water in the hallway; but she gradually grew used to it. Several days later the driver found out that a secretary-typist was required at the administration. Oleg's mother went to see about the job. The woman in charge of the meat-processing administration laughed at her surname, but, after checking the application and telephoning somewhere said: 'The main thing is that you're educated, you know – you can read and write.' And took her on to the staff.

In every letter, his father would ask whether their son was practising the violin regularly. Oleg's mother, in the long letters that she composed after putting the children to bed, would describe to her husband the miracle that had come to pass. 'Oleg plays more than ever now. I don't even have to make him do it, he enjoys it so much. It turns out that you and I weren't mistaken; he really does have talent. As soon as the war is over, you'll see for yourself.'.

Yes, the maestro played indeed, but there was nobody to give him lessons. Oleg stuck with the scales that he stubbornly repeated twenty times a day and the two primitive melodies.

'Take me to a music school,' he would ask. 'Papa told me to play the whole war through.'

'Where am I going to find a music school? There isn't one here ...'

There was neither orchestra nor musicians in the town, either. And even if there had been his mother wouldn't have been able to find them. People said that there had been a brass band that worked part-time playing for funerals, but all of them, under the direction of their fireman-conductor, had been sent off to the front. However, on the bank of the town's *prud*, or lake-sized mill-pond, just on the other side of the dam, nestled a little house surrounded by skinny poplars. A hundred and one years before the war, by the greatest of fortuities, Peter Ilich Tchaikovsky himself had been born there. Since it was the only institution in the whole neighbourhood with any relation to music, his mother set off for the small house by the dam in search of a teacher.

The house Tchaikovsky had been born in wasn't big, and it had little windows facing out on to the front garden and a little porch. A memorial museum to the composer had been set up within it.

There were no visitors to the museum, apparently; people weren't up to it. The custodian and director of the museum turned out to be, according to the plaque on the door, a Comrade Chupeyev. His mother saw a spry old man with palsied hands and a moustache that reminded her of the cavalry general Budenny. When Chupeyev wanted to say something, he would first lick his moustache, which would end up in his mouth and then fly back out again with his words. The old man's wall eyes would water and gaze in two different directions, as if avoiding the person he was speaking to.

His mother explained the purpose of her visit to him at length and incoherently, but he couldn't understand what she was on about.

'Speak louder, I'm hard of hearing!' the director would demand every now and again.

Oleg's mother repeated everything from the beginning, and this time it looked as though he got it.

'There aren't any violinists in our town, you know. None, that's the way of it. I myself hacked up the Whites in our neighbourhood with my sabre, at the trot. And now here I am on a meritorious pension. But since there's a war on, I've come out to answer the call on the cultural front . . .'

The director tore a square from a newspaper and rolled himself a smoke, using coarse black *makhorka* tobacco, and then deftly struck himself a light with flint and steel, lighting up from the smouldering wick.

Oleg's mother started coughing from the fumes. The words that she pronounced were orchestrated from a distance by her husband, who had already been drafted into the militia, and she wouldn't retreat, she couldn't retreat.

'My husband is at the front. He told me to teach my son music. And you don't want to help me!'

'The front is everywhere now,' Chupeyev said sternly, understanding her words as a reproach. 'However, I, too, was put here to guard our cultural achievements and not just for fun . . . And besides, little mother, I'm hard of hearing.'

Oleg's mother wouldn't give up.

'Since you're the only one in this town who works around music, help me. The boy is a prodigy, do you understand?'

'A prodda-what?'

'You know, a genius. What else can we do? After all, everything is going to be over soon, we'll be going home, and our Oleg will go back to his music school again. But for now . . . I wouldn't ask you to do it for nothing!'

'There's a war on, my dear.' The old man tried to justify his stance. 'Money doesn't come into it. It's too bad, of course, for the boy. Well . . . What can we do? All right. Let him come over.'

Oleg's mother ran home joyfully.

'Son, I've found you a music teacher after all! I found one! Only you have to play louder for him, he's a little bit deaf.'

Towards evening Oleg took his violin and set off for the museum behind the dam, to the old man. The museum was already closed, and Oleg had to knock at the door.

'Well, now, let me have a look at your fiddle!' said Chupeyev, letting Oleg in.

The maestro glanced around. Inside, it was in semi-darkness; on the walls there were portraits in antique frames, on the tables sheets of music were spread, under glass. The old man turned the violin over in his hands with curiosity, smoking it up with his *makhorka* to the extent that the smell would exude from its f-holes for long afterwards. Without taking the bow in his hands, the director tried the strings with his thumb, returned the violin and said: 'All right. You don't have to be God to fire a clay pot. Tune it up, lad.'

He sat down in an armchair that Tchaikovsky's father had sat in regally when the great composer himself was Oleg's age and studying music.

'A,' Nemets junior requested.

'What was that?' the music teacher failed to hear.

'Play A for me, please.'

The old man obediently went over to the grand piano standing in a corner of the room, wiped the dust off the keyboard cover with his palm and wiped it against his rear end. He raised the cover and with one finger played the scale from C to C, the only thing that the director could do. Oleg caught his A, tuned his violin quickly and waited.

'Well, go ahead.' The old man let out a cloud of smoke. 'What can you reproduce?'

Oleg had several pieces that he could sight-read. But that music had been left behind in the confusion of their departure. There had been no time for that sort of thing when they were evacuating. Oleg was beginning to cough from the smoke, but he raised the violin to his chin.

'I can play exercises for each string and for all of them . . . some études, too.'

'And can you play something from a ready-made piece?'

'I can do Beethoven's "Marmot".'

'"Marmot?" Good grief, then, go ahead with your marmot.'

The old man approached him from the side, bent his head closer to the violin and began to roll another cigarette. Oleg liked Beethoven's

'Marmot'. He would sing it even when he wasn't playing. '*I wandered throughout diff'rent lands / My marmot right beside me . . .*'

You had to feel sorry for the marmot. Homeless, downtrodden and hungry, it wandered with its master in search of a piece of bread. Oleg would keep 'The Marmot' in his memory for his entire life and sing it to his son a quarter of a century later.

Nemets junior played 'The Marmot' twice through, began for the third time and then stopped. Lowering his violin, he stood in silence except for his coughing at the *makhorka* smoke.

'Good boy,' Chupeyev praised him. 'And do you know the song "Holy War"?'

'I do. Only I can't play it.'

'Then sing it. Only really loud, since I'm hard of hearing.'

'Arrrise, grrrreat land,' Oleg burst into song, '*rrrise up forrrr the fatal fight!*'

'Hey, you don't sing too badly either!' the old man exclaimed. 'You must learn to play "Holy War" by next time. And it'd be nice to do "The Internationale" as well. But that marmot, marmot . . . There's a war on. Got to fight! That's enough for today. As soon as you learn them, come on over. And we'll sing them together.'

Oleg thought that 'The Marmot' was music for wartime anyway. He had seen a lot of homeless and hungry people at the railway stations. But Nemets wasn't about to argue. He buttoned up his silver violin cover. The old man shook his hand goodbye, as if Oleg were a grown-up, and propelled him towards the door.

It was the beginning of autumn. It had already got dark on the street. A chill wind blew off the lake to meet him, rustling the poplar branches and carrying off the dry leaves. The streetlights weren't on. A piece of the moon glimmered across the water. Oleg quickened his pace then started to run for home. A kiosk stood where the dam ended. According to the sign on it, ice cream had been for sale there before the war. Oleg had already passed the stall when he was jerked to one side by his collar. He had no chance to work out what was happening before he was grabbed by the shoulders, spun around and pressed against the stall wall. He hugged his violin with both arms.

'Got anything to smoke?'

'But . . . I don't smoke – '

There were five of them, and the eldest were two heads taller than he was. They looked at him, squinting their eyes and giggling, nudging each other with their shoulders in encouragement.

'Well, then, got any readies?'

He didn't have any money either. But they themselves cleared that up, going through his pockets.

'Wotcher got, then?' asked the one standing opposite him, who was the ringleader.

He dexterously rolled his cigarette with his lips from right to left and back again.

'Poke him in the eye, Crosseyes, and have him clear off,' someone suggested.

So it was Crosseyes. The whole town was afraid of him. He was the one who would take the bread off children when they were running home after queuing for it. Oleg knew that in a situation like this crying was the worst thing to do – but the tears were running by themselves, either from helplessness or just from fright.

Crosseyes' gaze alighted on the silver violin cover.

'What's with the little suitcase? Take a look at it, Shotglass.'

Shotglass, small and brisk, darted from under Crosseyes.

'Hey, this is Nemets, the pluck-out. Nemets – he's got a name like that. Fascist, you know; Fritz . . .'

'Great!' Crosseyes brayed. 'Means we got ourselves a fascist prisoner. Maybe we'll string him up, eh?'

Everyone chattered. Shotglass, meanwhile, grabbed at the violin cover. Oleg hugged the violin with both arms.

'Hear that order?' squeaked Shotglass. 'Well, then!'

Now they were going to take it, and then . . . His father would never forgive his mother, and his mother would never forgive Oleg. He was done for.

'Got a German mug on him, but he walks around on our Russian soil.'

Crosseyes lazily took a step forward and casually stretched out his fist. But he missed Oleg's nose and hit him on the cheekbone instead, under his eye. The pain made Oleg think faster. Not knowing yet quite what to do, he squeezed his violin tighter. Suddenly he, shortest of all of them, squatted down sharply, as if he had vanished below and, clutching the violin to his stomach, darted headfirst between Crosseyes' legs. Crosseyes tried to trip him up, but Oleg was already on the ground anyway. They didn't have a chance to pile on to him. Another moment and he had crawled out of the circle and was sneaking into the shadows, into the bushes.

'Catch that fascist!' It was Crosseyes' voice.

'Don't worry!' the others reassured him 'He ain't going far.' The company spread out to comb the surroundings.

Oleg was lying in the weeds at the fence, pressed to the ground, covering the violin with his body. His arms, face and legs were stinging from the nettles, everything burning, an unbearable pain seizing his body.

Crosseyes' pals circled and whistled, cursing, and gathered together at the stall. Then Oleg began crawling. He crawled on his belly, like the scouts in the pictures did. He failed, however, to sneak away.

'There he goes!' Shotglass howled joyfully.

The gang ran up and surrounded Nemets in a tight ring. He stood up, still hugging his violin with both arms.

Two strong hands prised his elbows apart. Shotglass snatched away the violin in its cover and held it out to Crosseyes. Crosseyes shifted his cigarette from one corner of his mouth to the other and ordered: 'Right, open it up! I'll have a look at this balalaika!'

Shotglass started trying to unfasten the violin cover. He didn't have any luck, so he just ripped the buttons off. Finally the cover slipped off, and the violin was left naked.

'Fine-looking job!' Crosseyes drawled with satisfaction, interestedly turning the instrument over in his hands. 'Well, then, fascist, play it! Let's have a listen!' And he held out the violin to Oleg.

Oleg took the instrument and shook his head. 'I don't know how. I'm only studying.'

Oleg picked up the cover from the ground and with shaking hands tried to pull it over the violin. It was torn out of his hands again and thrown into the mud.

'We *dee-sire* some music,' grinned Crosseyes. 'Am I talking the truth?'

The gang hooted animatedly.

'Play!'

Crosseyes held his fist up under Oleg's nose.

'You get what this smells like? Ha!' And everyone again burst out cackling after him.

Oleg would have started crying, but the skin on his face was burning so hard that the tears couldn't flow, or he just didn't feel them. And now the solution, as immediate and salty as tears, came to him. He understood clearly: he had no alternative. He threw the violin to the ground and stamped on it once, then another time, then a third. The violin made a horrible crunching noise. One string twanged under the sole of his shoe and then fell silent.

For several moments the gang was in limbo. Everyone looked at Crosseyes. Shotglass was the first one to take alarm.

'Crosseyes! Let's drown him in the lake . . .'

Oleg darted to one side. But they hit him and held his arms so that he couldn't make off.

'Patrol's coming!' shouted someone.

A military patrol was making its way across the dam, three strapping sailors in black pea coats with red armbands on their sleeves and machine-guns. Crosseyes was chickening out but pretended that he was just losing interest.

'Let him go! He's bonkers,' Crosseyes said.

He himself turned and disappeared in an instant. Somebody kicked Oleg in the rear, and they all scattered off in various directions, following the example of their chief. The patrol passed slowly by and disappeared into the darkness.

Left in solitude, Oleg bent down and picked up what used to be his violin from the ground. Chunks of the veneer hung from the strings. He carefully stuffed the pieces into the silver bag and slowly shuffled off home.

His mother was busy in the kitchen. Catching sight of the nettle-swollen face of her son and the bruise under his eye, she hugged Oleg; she keened over him, weeping. He said that he had been in a fight, and that was it: she couldn't find out anything else from him.

He hung the violin bag back on its nail as if nothing had happened to it. His eye began to swell and wouldn't open. A fierce grievance gripped his heart.

'When *is* your next class, son?' asked his mother from the kitchen.

'In three days,' answered Oleg.

For three days he lied to his mother on her return from work, telling her he had practised three times that day, that he was learning the songs 'Holy War' and 'The Internationale'. He didn't want his mother to worry and write about the incident to his father.

The bag with the remains of his violin hung above his bed. Lyuska guessed what was going on, God knows how: Oleg didn't even manage to rush over to his fiddle when she pulled the bag from its nail and opened it up. Splinters and tangled strings fell out.

'That's just what I thought,' drawled Lyuska philosophically. But she didn't tell on Oleg.

It seemed to him that his mother was glad that he was practising. And Oleg now and again thought about that moment when she would find out that the violin didn't exist any longer. If only she could find out sooner!

'You know, Oleg,' his mother said to him one evening. 'Today some scum took Lyuska's bread away from her on the dam. Our host grabbed his axe and I ran along with him, but there was nobody there any more.'

'That's Crosseyes! I know it's Crosseyes!' shouted Oleg and fell silent.

'Our neighbour told me it was Crosseyes, too. But how's your music coming along?'

'You see, the teacher told me to tell you that I was very talented. He just doesn't have anything to teach me. He said that I could be a Paganini, perhaps, or maybe even an Oistrakh. But after the war.'

His mother sank into a chair and stared at her son in amazement.

'By God, you're as much a freak as your father is! Only . . . he's never lied to me.'

Nemets junior glanced at the nail above his bed. There was nothing there.

'Where's my violin?' he asked.

'My dear God, of course I've thrown it away!' his mother shook her head. 'There you are.'

'I didn't say anything to her,' Lyuska said, just in case.

'But how did you find out, Mum?'

His mother tightened her lips so as not to burst into tears at all that had happened to her recently and so often. She pulled a piece of the carved bridge of the violin out of her pocket.

'Here's a souvenir for you.'

'Where did you get it from?'

'The morning after you were in your fight, as I was running to work. And there it was; I found it on the dam. We'll buy you another violin after the war. But when you write to your father, not a word about this, right?'

# THE GOUACHE BOX

Long before the war, Oleg's father had bought a box of expensive Japanese paints. This is the way it happened.

All his life Nemets senior had wanted to become an artist. As a youngster he had taken his sketches to the artist Grabar, and that worthy even praised him once. He even tried to make etchings, like Favorsky. Fate, evidently, was not on his side. He became a retoucher in a photo studio and then in a publishing house. There they needed more and more retouchers for touching up real life, which was getting better and better, happier and happier, in their books. But the dream of becoming a painter never died in his father's soul. The shade of the unrealized artist dogged his heels and once propelled him into an absurd deed.

His father was walking down a city-centre street, and in the brightly lit window of a *torgsin* (there once were such stores for trading in hard currency with foreigners and with their own citizens for solid gold jewellery) he saw some Japanese paints in a grey cardboard box. The box with blue hieroglyphs on its sides was open, and in it stood twenty-four little jars with royal coats of arms on their shiny nickel-plated caps. It would have been obvious even to a dilettante that to have such paints would make it impossible not to become an artist. While he stood at the window he realized: if he let such an opportunity slip by, it might never appear again. That box had to belong to him, no matter what the cost.

So he popped into the shop to have a go at getting hold of it. He addressed the salesgirl, but she openly laughed at him. They didn't sell anything in a *torgsin* for Soviet money. He walked out with nothing, upset at first, but on his way home he calmed down and gave in. That evening he told his wife about it, as a joke: a king's ransom not for a horse – what would he need a horse for? – but for some paints. But his wife reacted to the joke with unexpected seriousness.

'Wait! I have a gold ring, you know! Remember, my grandma gave it to me as a present when I met you . . .'

Her grandmother was sure that if Oleg's father saw the pure-gold ring he would marry the girl straight away. He really did marry her. True, he only saw the ring after the wedding. His wife was embarrassed about wearing it (at the time it wasn't the fashion in the proletarian state, to put it mildly), and, without saying anything to her grandmother, she had quietly hidden the ring away and then just forgotten about it in all the fuss.

But when she realized that her husband wanted the Japanese paints she rooted around for a while in her things and found the ring, hidden in an old purse where it had remained for several years, and held it out to him. He waved his hands in refusal.

'What do we need it for?' she exclaimed. 'A knick-knack from the old days, that's all it is. Who'd take a notion to wear something like that now? Only the surviving bourgeoisie or former NEP profiteers. But paints are vitally important to us. With paints like that, you can create things and become a real artist. Then you'll see, you'll be in the Tretyakov Gallery!'

Oleg's mother didn't understand anything either about paints or painting, but she sensed the yearnings of his father's soul. His father, hesitating a moment, took the ring and set off for the *torgsin*.

There the receptionist lazily picked up a loupe and examined the hallmark on the inside, tossed the ring into a special balance and wrote something into the register.

'For recasting,' she said and threw the ring into a box sitting in the safe. 'What did you want to buy?'

'I'd like some paints,' he said. 'Th-those over there, the Japanese ones.'

She placed the box with the blue hieroglyphs on its side in front of him on the counter.

'Nothing else?'

'How much is left over?'

'Enough for some brushes,' she said.

Oleg's father hadn't expected such luck. A packet of brushes lay across the box.

His father carried the box into their home in front of him solemnly, as if he were performing some pagan ritual. His face was radiant.

'How much did it cost, then?' his wife asked, out of simple curiosity.

'If you find out, you'll divorce me,' he answered.

For as long as Oleg Nemets could recall, the box had sat on the shelf under the radio set. It was strictly forbidden to touch those paints. His father personally showed the gouaches to all the friends and acquaintances who frequented their home, setting out the jars with their brightly coloured labels one after the other on the table. He was very proud to have such paints.

It would have appeared that there was nothing special about the box: a dark-grey case made of heavy cardboard. Except perhaps for the intricate blue hieroglyphs inscribed on the sides. But then . . . inside! The jars with their bright paints standing six in a row, each in its special cusped niche. Like in a fun-house mirror, you could inspect your own contorted image in the nickel-plated caps. Ancient coats of arms stood out in relief on the caps. The paints' colours were pure, juicy. And, on top of all that, if you unscrewed the cap, you would get a whiff of its peculiar odour – tasty, even.

Oleg's father wanted to get away from the daily grind, to free himself up a little from working overtime and to take up painting again, as he had done in his youth. But this time in earnest. He didn't talk about it, but he thought about it a lot. They didn't have enough money to get by on, so he took on more and more work. Most likely, though, besides lacking money he lacked talent and persistence. But, in this case no less than any other, who would have taken the liberty to deny a man the right to hope?

So he never took the time to pick up his brushes and try his paints.

No, that's not true, though – he did open them up, once after the war began: the building manager came to the Nemetses' and asked him to paint him a sign saying 'Maintain the Blackout!' The sign came out really bright and eloquent. But he had never cracked open the paints again.

Later on Oleg often thought that it must have been his and Lyuska's fault that his father's dreams were never destined to come true. He and his sister had to be fed, clothed and shod; Oleg had to be taught music. Oleg and Lyuska were indubitably guilty already for being born. But not just them alone. And if not just them, who else? Hitler? Stalin? Destiny?

Mother and children were to be evacuated. Their father was staying behind alone. At a loss, he stood in the middle of their small room and looked around him. What else were they forgetting that was absolutely necessary?

'No matter!' he said, almost happily. 'It's not for long. You'll be back soon! But for me, this is what you have to take away. Only this. Who knows what . . . ?'

He handed the box with the Japanese paints over to his wife.

'Maybe when you're alone you'll start painting?' she carefully suggested.

'Now isn't the time for that, anyway. But they'll be safe with you.'

Father turned to son.

'Just watch out for my paints. Don't break them! The war will come to an end, and I'll definitely get down to painting. You'll see!'

Everyone was certain then that happiness would come along right after the war, all by itself, complete, bright, joyful, and everything would come true, come to pass, be realized instantly, like someone waving a magic wand.

So the box with the Japanese paints found its way into the plywood *Belomorkanal* cigarette crate that made its way to a town in the Ural mountains with Oleg and Lyuska and their mother. Their father stayed home. There, he was sent to the front. Here, all their cares fell to their mother.

At the flea market she sold all the good clothes that they had brought with them, piece by piece. She patched up their old clothes for herself and the children. Then there was nothing left to sell. Several times she took the grey box with the paints out of the crate, turned it around in her fingers and then hid it away again.

But, one day, when it had become even harder to get food, she hesitantly added on to the end of a letter to her husband: 'I also wanted to ask you about the Japanese paints. What if we traded them for some bran or a piece of suet? The war will end, and we'll buy some new ones, a hundred times better than these.'

No answer came.

Their mother worried, cursed herself for writing to her husband about the paints. After all, he was going to take up painting after the war. Why the hell had she bothered him with it?

Once Lyuska and her mother were sent to the country to dig potatoes for three days. Oleg stayed home alone. Straight away he gobbled down everything that his mother had left him to eat for the whole time. On the second day Oleg was starving, and on the third he remembered about the paints.

He took them out from the bottom of the plywood crate and carried them off to the market. Now he would exchange them for bread and food, fill himself up and feed his mother and Lyuska as well when they came back. At the part of the market that was set aside for the *tolkuchka*, the flea market, the joint was definitely not jumping. There people were walking around unhurriedly, stopping, inspecting the goods, asking prices, bargaining. The people who were selling something or offering things for barter stood in rows, calling out:

'Who wants new riding breeches? Almost-new riding breeches . . .'

'Pre-war calico. Step up, little ladies!'

'A German map-case! Was German, now Soviet!'

'Old boots, you fix 'em, they'll be brand new!'

Oleg joined the line with his Japanese paints.

A lot of people came up to him. They would take the box, open it up, inspect the royal coats of arms on the nickel-plated caps, get surprised by their distorted reflections, hold the paints up to the light, shake them for some reason, even lick them, trying their taste. Some smirked, some clucked their tongues, some asked from where the young owner had stolen the box, some shrugged their shoulders, but everyone returned the paints to him without asking how much or what Oleg wanted in return for them.

He stood like that for half a day. Then, disheartened, completely famished, he took the paints home and hid them back in their place. The pit of his stomach was aching with hunger. He ate some potato peelings that he had fished out of his neighbours' bin. He cooked them in a skillet, now and again pouring in more water.

He said nothing to his mother when she and Lyuska came back.

About a quarter of a century had passed since that time.

One day Oleg Nemets came home. He glanced into the room from the entry hall and saw his son drawing and talking to himself. Oleg sat down beside him, to make head or tail of the drawings. In the pictures tanks crawled forward, cannons were firing, aeroplanes were swooping and, of course, rockets were taking off with fluffy fiery tails.

'What's that?' asked Oleg.

'Can't you see? A dogfight! These are our lads, and these are the fascists. Fire! Kapow, kapow . . .'

Oleg couldn't tell which were our lads and which the fascists. But, really, some sort of battle was going on in the picture, and Valesha knew exactly who was where. From where would a child, born a decade and a half after the war and not knowing how to read, get such wide historical information? Evidently, partly from kindergarten, as well as from children's books and from watching television besides. Here, there and everywhere they endlessly told and retold and showed the war.

But Valesha was, in general, a strange child. Once, angry with his mother for an unfair reproach, he snatched a fat red pencil and drew a line along the whole length of the wall. When Oleg asked him what was depicted on the wallpaper, his son answered, already calmed down: 'Can't you tell? That's my anger!'

His wife was indignant, but Oleg was curious. He told his brother-in-law Nefyodov about this 'line of anger'. How would Lyuska's husband explain his spirited son's behaviour?

Nefyodov, a teacher of history in school, a major couch philosopher, thought for a bit and then interpreted the fact in his own way. 'It's probably self-expression,' he said. 'The boy is trying to find himself by depicting something . . . If you want to teach your son how to paint, don't buy him those little children's paint boxes. Buy him jars of real gouache, big brushes, let him slather it on whatever he likes, however he likes. Don't truss up his imagination. They'll have plenty of time yet to truss it up.'

Nemets did just that. He bought a roll of wallpaper and tacked big pieces of it around the walls, with the plain side out. It would be better to let Valesha express his feelings here than to redecorate the apartment.

'Draw everywhere,' Oleg ordered him. 'But, in fact, what you need is real paints. I'll get some on payday.'

'Buy me some,' his son agreed. 'Grandmother's wanted to give me some as a present for a long time but never has.'

Oleg had also noticed that his mother had got considerably older in the last few years and forgetful.

'Did you promise him some paints?' Oleg asked, when she dropped by for a visit.

'That's right, I did! Our paints, Father's, remember . . . ?'

From time to time, Oleg's mother would find and give some of her keepsakes to her grandson as a present: now an 'Honourable Donor' badge, now some playing cards, now a fifty-kopek coin from some superseded coinage. And, sure enough, the next time she came by she hadn't forgotten: she had brought a package with her.

Oleg unwrapped it and looked over the half-disintegrated carton with its faded blue hieroglyphs for a long time.

'You know what, Mum? I actually took these to sell them once . . .'

'I know,' his mother nodded. 'I did, too, son. But who cared about Japanese paints in those days? That's why nobody bought them. So where's Valesha?'

Her grandson was lying under the bed with a wooden machine-gun in his hands, tracking enemies of some sort.

'Valesha!' she called. 'Come here!'

Solemnly holding the grey box in front of her, his grandma intoned: 'Here are the paints. Remember, the ones I promised? Paint me that battle with the fascists, the one I told you about.' The location of at least one source of information from which the child drew his knowledge of that wretched war was now known.

'Valesha,' added his grandmother, 'these are your granddad's paints. Look after them! These are good paints, Japanese gouache. Isn't that right, Olya?'

'Who's Olya?' asked Valesha.

'Olya is your father,' said his grandma. 'I called him Olya when he was little.'

'Very funny,' noted Valesha. 'What was he, a girl?'

'Spit and image of your grandpa!' said his grandmother. 'He would always say "Very funny!" But he wouldn't laugh.'

'Gran, where's my grandfather?' asked Valesha.

Oleg's mother blinked her eyes, not answering.

'Will he come to see us?'

'No, he won't,' said Oleg dully.

'Never?'

He got no answer, and Valesha didn't ask again. He had already opened the box. There stood the twenty-four multi-hued jars – the nickel-plated caps with their coats of arms slightly faded but still reflecting objects. Oleg handed his son a brush and silently pointed at the piece of paper on the wall.

'Open them up,' his son softly requested.

Oleg tried to unscrew the caps. Their edges had rusted tight and wouldn't budge. Nemets whacked them with his fist, wrapped a damp rag around them, poured hot water on them and, finally, soaking the caps in eau-de-Cologne, managed to unscrew them.

The paints in their jars remained as bright as they had been before, but they had turned hard over the years, their surfaces all cracks. Valesha wasn't going to paint with these.

'Dad,' as before, his son asked in a whisper, 'buy me some other ones, that I can paint with. You promised, after all . . .'

'Well, how are the paints?' his grandmother yelled from the kitchen. 'Do you like them?'

'Very much, thanks!' answered her grandson.

Wordlessly, Oleg noted proudly how nice it was to be around well-bred people.

'Oleg, I think it's time to teach Valesha music . . .'

The next day he went to the department store and stood for a while looking at the violins. His mother's good intentions of making her favourite grandson saw away on the fiddle were understandable. But one violinist – himself – at home was enough. So Nemets took home a bag stuffed full of multicoloured jars of paint from the store. It would be better to have a painter at home: at least it would be quiet.

The new paints were put to use at once. Valesha straight away started to paint aeroplanes, tanks and yet other things, understandable to him alone, on the walls.

'When war comes,' his son explained, 'I'll fly in this kind of rocket. Look!' And he pointed at the wall.

'The only thing we haven't got is a war,' muttered Oleg's wife. 'And you'd be there flying around in it . . .'

'Well, of course, in a rocket,' Oleg agreed. 'What else would you be in?'

'War is very interesting, isn't it?' asked his son.

'Not very,' said Nemets.

He put the dried Japanese paints carefully into their box and placed it on the sideboard.

'Is Valesha still painting?' his grandmother would ask, dropping by their place for a visit.

'Of course he is! Here, you see?'

Oleg would point at the walls, hung with painted sheets of paper, and then look at the sideboard where the box of dried-up Japanese gouaches sat.

# LESSONS IN SILENCE

The bus set off in a tired sort of way. From behind Oleg an old woman tried to hang on to the glassless door with weak fingers. The door closed and squeezed the woman tight against the passengers standing on the steps. Right in front of Oleg's eyes a hand, as narrow as if two had been made out of one, lay on the handrail. Suddenly Oleg felt hungry, although he had just eaten breakfast. The hand was holding a silver spoon, full of sugar, in front of his eyes. His mouth began to taste the sweetness.

At the next stop the doors inched apart with difficulty. It was getting light. Oleg saw a mole on the woman's cheek, near her nose – a large mole, which gave her face a laughing expression. The woman gazed past him, busy with her own thoughts. He tried quickly to find something to say if she recognized him, too. He had been eight years old then, and now, for all that, he had reached forty. Therefore she was . . .

At the long break she would go and get a loaf of bread for the whole class from the caretaker, cut it into slices and divide up the slices into quarters. Slowly she would walk down the aisle and place three pieces on every desk. Then she would go around the class again and sprinkle out a teaspoonful of coarse yellow sugar for everyone from a linen bag. The starving children would greedily follow her long, narrow hand with their eyes. The spoon would quickly dip down into the bag, be carefully drawn out and then get tucked away again.

Everyone would start eating together when the emptied bag lay on the teacher's desk. Oleg would first nibble the shiny black edges unhurriedly. Sucking off the burned crust, he would gradually get closer and closer to the sugar. Now he could dip his tongue into the sugar and suck up the nectar, like a bee, grain by grain, strengthening his will in the interludes, so it would last longer.

The teacher was entitled to some bread and a teaspoonful of sugar, too. On the first day of the school year, out of inexperience, everyone ate theirs too fast and then fixed their gaze on her. She wiped her fingers with a handkerchief, sat down behind her desk and arranged her portion of bread in front of her. She lifted the piece to her mouth, but then raised her head and looked around the class instead: 'Who wants some more?'

All but one flung their hands up.

'How about you, Patrikeyeva?' the teacher asked.

Oleg glanced around. Patrikeyeva sat behind him, a sharp-cheek-boned Udmurt girl with wide-spaced eyes. Her mother was dead, and she knew nothing about her father. Before starting school she had lived in the country with her granny, and didn't understand Russian very well.

'Patrikeyeva,' the teacher said slowly, separating one word from the other. 'Why – don't – you – want – some – more?'

'I *do* wan' some!' Patrikeyeva thrust her arm up as well.

'All right, then. We'll have one extra piece. You will all get it in turn.'

'Wha' 'bout you?'

'I'm full, little ones. I don't want any . . .'

And then and there she brought the piece of bread to the first lucky one, and the whole class looked at her enviously.

Now every day at the long break the class would yell in chorus whose turn it was to be and, mouths watering, watch the one whose turn it was suck up their second portion.

But they probably loved her for another reason.

Oleg jogged his memory and with difficulty recalled her name, although usually names never stayed in his head. She had told them to call her Dasha Viktorovna, saying that the name on her passport was too difficult to pronounce and that she didn't like it anyway.

That year Oleg had been all set to go to a different school in a different city, where that spring his parents had applied for a place for him, but now he found himself in this one, because in between the two schools lay the evacuation. This school in the town near the Urals was a single-storeyed log cabin under black shingles, while the former real school down the street had been turned into a hospital. 'Oleg Nemets' – Dasha Viktorovna had entered the boy's name in her rounded handwriting, like the links of a chain, in her daybook.

The schoolyard, from fence to fence, was naked, stamped thoroughly flat. A few wary hanks of grass straggled out on the edges from under the boards of the fence, with its gaping chinks. They had made a shortcut to the school: they would run down between people's allotments, snacking on other people's carrots. The classrooms were small: the teacher's little desk, squeezed up against the warped, cracked blackboard, and the two-seater school desks of various sizes, at which the children sat hunched up, three at a desk. The schoolbag of the child in the middle would rest on the floor. Oleg propped his legs up on his. To let the child in the middle get to the blackboard, the child at one end or the other had to get up. Everyone would jump up eagerly: their bodies would have got numb, and they wanted to move.

Dasha Viktorovna looked as if the war hadn't touched her. Just as if she were living before it or after it. She wore a light-blue dress that clung to her figure and a lace-trimmed white blouse, like a stewardess today. Her face had high cheekbones, and her eyes slanted somewhat. Her dark, thick hair, combed perfectly back, was twisted into a tight knot, so tight that it seemed to Oleg that it always must have hurt.

After writing something in chalk on the blackboard she would carefully wipe her long fingers on a snow-white, lace-trimmed handkerchief and then fold it back up the way it had been previously. She was strikingly beautiful in profile, when she would glance out of the window, where beyond the glass with its frost patterns the ruddy dawn would be breaking. Her handwriting in the students' notebooks was as beautiful as she was herself.

No one in the world had time for anything, but she treated her children tenderly. Her blood could be running cold from what she had just read in the papers, never mind about what she might have heard, but she would read them fairy-tales and tie up their earflaps under their chins. Everyone's faces were sad – but she would be smiling in class. Or maybe the mole under her nose made her look happy?

She didn't like talking about herself. Only once did she recall the two happiest days of her life. On 20 June 1941 she had graduated from her teachers' training school, and on the 21st she had married a flight-school student. It had been planned long before, and at last had come to pass. They became husband and wife. He had flown off on the 22nd.

In November . . . no, in December of 1941 the frost was ferocious, below minus thirty degrees Celsius. In better times they would have been repeating over the radio that children didn't have to go to school. In the morning, running up to school before daybreak, Oleg could hear the screech of a saw. The caretaker Gaynulla would be shoving logs on to a sawhorse with his shoulder and setting to work with a two-handled saw, having rigged up a clever spring at the other end.

Gaynulla handled the job with only one arm. The flat right sleeve of his officer's tunic was tucked under his worn belt. His collar was open, one earflap of his hat was up, the other hung down. He didn't freeze even when it was thirty below, only a small cloud of steam hung around his face. Gaynulla worked frenziedly. The saw, set badly, would stick, he would jerk on it, digging his knee into the log. The log would rumble but wouldn't give up the saw.

Gawkers would crowd around the sawhorse until the very moment the bell rang. Some of them would offer advice on the best way to free the jammed saw blade, how to hold the saw. Whenever Gaynulla was sawing, it seemed as though he never noticed anyone around him. He was generally silent anyway and spoke only in extremis. He didn't even swear, except when the saw got stuck. After all, there were children around – he knew a little bit about teaching, too.

Everyone thought the caretaker was a soldier back from the front and, being rather afraid of him, treated him with respect. After all, he was like many of the students' fathers, who were far away. Not much older. But then on one occasion Gaynulla had told them how he had never been at the front. His arm had been cut off by a tram-wheel, before the war.

'So where's your tunic from?' Like flies, the children pestered him.

'I got the tunic. At the flea market. Brought some fatback from the village and traded for it.'

The respect melted away, and the caretaker became just a second-rate person, an adjunct of the school. Of course, he had to fetch firewood from the forest, stoke the two stoves whose sides each adjoined four classrooms, then saw more wood and ring the bell for break and classes.

Gaynulla would quietly steal into class with an armful of pine kindling smelling of pitch and noiselessly open the stove door, trying to remain unnoticed. If one of the chunks of wood fell to the floor because of him being one-armed, he would glance up at the teacher shamefacedly. After that, Gaynulla would run along the slippery street to the other end of town to the bakery, where with his dirty chit he would get four loaves of bread and a small bag of yellow sugar, after signing for it.

Gaynulla's irreplaceability made itself felt when he disappeared.

The fourth-grade teacher, muffled in a shawl, stepped out on to the porch with the bell. Ringing it, she passed the children through the door, lamenting: 'Oh, you little darlings of mine! You'll get frozen now. Where on earth has that Gaynulla got to . . . ?'

'He's took sick,' Patrikeyeva said.

'Fallen ill!' the teacher corrected her, sighing.

The teachers themselves brought in armfuls of firewood, ran in turn to the bakery for bread. The stoves would smoke, the children cough. A week later the firewood ran out. Gaynulla was in bed with pneumonia.

Usually, Dasha Viktorovna would come earlier than anyone,

before daylight, and sit in the warm classroom. She would correct homework up to the very bell, from time to time exchanging a couple of words with Gaynulla. The children would say hello, and she would mechanically nod to everyone, not taking her eyes off the notebooks. Now she didn't hurry to get there early, though; she appeared just before the bell.

The children sat in their overcoats, shoving their hats into their desks. It was far too crowded for three of them to sit behind a desk in their overcoats, but it was warmer. They would lean into each other, tucking their hands inside their collars. They would take them out when they had to write something down, and then they would hide them again.

One morning they discovered that the ink in everyone's wells had frozen.

'Never mind!' Dasha Viktorovna comforted them. 'Now our caretaker will be getting better soon, and it'll be warm again . . .'

The following day the fourth-grade teacher had long since rung the bell on the porch, but Dasha still hadn't shown up. Finally the door opened, and Dasha Viktorovna stood unmoving in the doorway in her overcoat with its fox-fur collar, tucked up so that the worn parts wouldn't be visible.

Everyone stood up heavily, sliding out from behind their desks with difficulty, and stood cheerfully while she slowly came up to her desk and stood still. A light cloud of steam appeared and disappeared around her mouth. Dasha leaned on the desk on her fists, looking past the class, at the wall. She was staring fixedly at a single point, and the children began to stir: what could she see, there on the back wall? Desks were squeaking, someone was breathing heavily, someone else shoved his neighbour, but she stood unmoving.

Outside, a sledge whooshed past, and the crack of the whip and a yell of 'Hey, up!' carried through the windows. And then everything was silent once again.

Dasha Viktorovna made an effort to pull herself together. She took out her handkerchief, already crushed and wet, covered her eyes with it, sat there. She wanted to say something, but the words wouldn't come.

The young teacher didn't give them permission to sit down, and no one knew how to act. Some children sat down by themselves, some continued to stand, leaning their elbows on their desks. The rickety benches creaked from time to time. Thin clouds of steam took wing from childish mouths. The silence seemed endless. All of a sudden, from behind Oleg, Patrikeyeva sobbed and burst into tears, throwing herself on to her desk. Everyone stared at her vacantly. She was a strange girl, gloomy and silent.

Soon Patrikeyeva calmed down and sat up, smearing her tears with her hands, all stained with ink, whose purple washed on to her face, making her look bruised. It became quiet again. Everyone sat without moving, afraid to look at each other and at Dasha Viktorovna, frozen in front of them but not there. They just sat with their noses buried in their desks. The bell rang for break, then for the second period. No one moved from their places.

Suddenly, in the middle of the second period, Gaynulla entered the classroom with an armful of firewood. Usually when Gaynulla came in the children didn't stand up, but here, all of a sudden, everyone rose – from nervous tension perhaps. He was emaciated, his face was covered with stubble, there was snow on his hat, beads of sweat on his forehead. He had come to work still sick. He looked like a decrepit old man, a goner.

The caretaker stopped at the door and looked at Dasha, his lips moving. He dumped the wood, sighed heavily, sat down on his haunches and adroitly pulled some kindling and a home-made lighter out of his back pocket. He stacked the firewood, put the kindling under it and set it alight. The cold stove started smoking; the wood didn't want to burn. The smoke crawled along the ceiling to the windows and descended, looking for an exit. The class began to cough. But gradually the fire took, and the stove began to draw, pulling the air back into itself, the wood beginning to flame.

Leaving, Gaynulla turned around, looked at Dasha again, shook his head and quietly pulled the door to behind him. Towards the end of the second period the caretaker returned. Coughing resonantly, he stuffed the stove full of wood once more and again disappeared.

He appeared again during the long break. He stumbled into the room, breathing heavily, and put a loaf of bread and a small bag of sugar on the table in front of Dasha. She nodded, not looking at him, and he, without a word, pulled a penknife out of his tunic pocket and opened it with his one left hand, catching the tip of the blade on the edge of her desk and, skilfully trapping the loaf under his stomach, began to slice it.

Dasha Viktorovna came to her senses, opened her briefcase, took her silver spoon out and put it in front of Gaynulla. He beckoned Patrikeyeva with a finger. He spooned up the sugar, sprinkled it over the bread, and Patrikeyeva carried them around to the desks. Their customary ritual had been ruined: he was supposed to hand out the bread first, and then pass along the desks to sprinkle out the sugar, so that not a grain was spilled on the floor.

As usual, the last piece should have been given to the pupil next in line as an extra. Rather large, the piece lay on the table.

'Eat it up, Dasha Wiktorobna,' Patrikeyeva said quietly. She always pronounced the patronymic strangely.

'Eat it,' Patrikeyeva repeated. 'Nobody wants it.'

'Thanks.'

Barely moving her lips, their teacher pronounced her first word of the day and raised the piece to her mouth. The one whose turn it was to get the piece that day opened his mouth to remind her of it but kept his silence. Her hand was shaking, the sugar spilled over her desk. She ate it, then out of inertia swept the crumbs up and poured them into her mouth, took out her wet handkerchief, pressed it to her lips and sat motionless.

When the bell rang at the end of the third period, Dasha said, her voice breaking at every word, as if the words were being squeezed out of her throat in spasms: 'Go . . . out . . . to break. Go . . . on. Go.'

She wasn't ashamed of her tears any more.

The ones who were closest to the door got up first. They slipped out into the corridor, leaving the door ajar. Behind them, with a noise like chickens leaving their roost, the rest leaped out of their desks, their coat-tails flapping.

The class quickly emptied. Everyone stood in the corridor, crowding around, not understanding anything, and for that reason not daring to rush around and fight as usual. The fourth-grade teacher, muffled in her shawl, came up to the crowd.

'Well, how's your Dasha Viktorovna doing? You'd better not upset her, children. She's had a misfortune. His plane was shot down. Her husband . . . Anyway, a death notice arrived.'

They stood there in a crowd until the bell rang and went back into the classroom. Patrikeyeva hadn't left the class, as it turned out. They took their places again and sat, not talking, not arguing, not fighting. It got gradually warmer in the classroom, and the smoke less. The pupils silently rose and hung their overcoats on the nails driven into a plank on the wall. Dasha alone sat in her overcoat. She felt a chill.

When classes were over, she let them go and stayed behind alone.

Next morning Oleg was afraid to go to school and wanted to stay at home. His mother, running off to work, threatened to write to his father at the front. Although they hadn't received any news from him for a long time, and this was a hoary old device, it still worked for some reason.

Behind the school fence the saw was working away more animatedly than usual. The path through the gates had already been swept clean, and smoke was cheerfully entwined around the roof. In the yard on the other side of the sawhorse, opposite the caretaker, stood Dasha Viktorovna, her overcoat unbuttoned. Oleg looked cautiously at her. Her face was red, she was out of breath. And those who had come to school in fear took heart and joyfully sprang up the stairs.

Dasha Viktorovna left off sawing and ran after the children. It was quiet during classes but not like it had been the day before. Their teacher had taken herself in hand or maybe distracted herself sawing the wood. Her eyes remained cold and alien, but she spoke, even smiled a little bit.

The class came back to life. That day everyone tried to sit without fidgeting and to read and write with all their hearts, even the constant fidgeters like the pugnacious Stasik, who sat in front of Oleg. Dasha usually said that, after the war, when there would be roomy classrooms and desks enough for all, she would put Stasik all by himself. Stasik lived with his mother and four sisters. A death notice for his father had come at the very beginning of the war.

Days passed, and Dasha Viktorovna gradually returned to her old self. Winter was yielding. The sun would come out from behind the clouds for a little while. Stamping hooves made ruts that the water would freeze in towards evening, and, with a little run-up, you could slide around the entire neighbourhood.

One evening, Oleg and his friends were hanging out on the street. They shucked sunflower seeds, pushed one another, chased after an overloaded sledge. Hanging off the transom, they skated along behind the sledge until the driver they had sneaked up on chased them off with his whip. They would have gone to the pictures – A Girl with Character was showing – but no one had any money.

'Looky there!' Stasik suddenly shouted and pointed his finger at the other side of the street.

Dasha Viktorovna was walking along the duckboard pavement there. Now she was surely going to run across the street to find out what her pupils were doing here and send them all home. But Dasha didn't pay any attention to them. Alongside her strode Gaynulla, proudly sticking out in front of him his new hand, in a black glove.

It wasn't the prosthesis that surprised everybody – the caretaker had been walking around classes with his prosthetic hand for three days already, carrying wood. If the wooden billets resisted going into the stove in any way he would shove them in with his wooden hand.

He let the children push the lever on it: the spring would snap, and the arm would bend up on its own. No, it had nothing to do with the prosthesis – but with the fact that their teacher was arm in arm with Gaynulla. And it was not the prosthesis that he was carrying so solemnly in front of him, but her live hand, lying on his artificial one.

They stopped in front of the picture theatre, looked at the poster and passed on. And her pupils stood as if rooted to the ground, following after them with their eyes.

'Did you see that? So that's how it is!'

In imitation of them, Stasik waddled down the street, holding his arm the way Gaynulla did his.

'Well, what was there to see?' asked Oleg.

'What, you mean you didn't see what a whore she is? Her husband just gets killed, but her, that bitch, she's already going out with another bloke!'

They suddenly didn't feel like messing around outside any longer, and it was getting cold anyway. Hunched over, they all straggled back to their homes.

The next day Oleg entered the classroom but stopped just inside the door.

'You heard about Dasha?' the excited Stasik, standing on top of his desk, jumped down on to the floor and grabbed Nemets by his shirt collar. 'Although . . . you were with us, anyway . . .'

He had already spread yesterday's news to everyone in class, but Oleg had seen everything yesterday for himself, and Stasik lost interest in him.

It was as if the class had been switched with a different one. It was some kind of mass hysteria, call it whatever you like. Everyone, including the quietest girls, was leaping from desk to desk, fighting, meowing. Oleg threw his bag down under his desk and, in order not to get left behind, started throwing his fur hat into the air and catching it. The hat caromed off the ceiling, falling back, showering Oleg with white dust and turning white itself. Yelling, Stasik shifted the desks around, and soon it was impossible to move anywhere in the classroom.

Nobody noticed when Dasha came in. No, of course they had noticed; that was why it got even noisier. She leaned against the doorway, turned pale, wanted to say something, but it was useless. She couldn't shout down everyone at once, so she quietly forced her way through the desks, which had been moved to make a sort of barricade, towards her teacher's desk, found her up-ended chair, put it back into its place and sat down. Dasha looked out at what was going on, her eyes wide, and waited.

Stasik was jumping up on to his desk and then sitting down again. He would jump up, turn his bum to the teacher and shake it and then sit down on the desk again. He put his hands to his mouth, forming them into a tube, and then trumpeted or, rather, roared out something loud and nonsensical.

Dasha sat patiently, not understanding what was going on, and simply waited for the class to get tired and calm down. Far from it.

'But, I thought . . .' she began.

No one was interested in what she thought. They weren't listening to her or pretended not to be listening to her.

Finally they got tired of yelling and running around, it seemed. They needed a breather, maybe, or had simply got bored. Then Dasha told them to open their notebooks. Some opened theirs; the majority didn't.

Their teacher asked: 'Nemets, did you do your homework?'

Chalk was still coming from Oleg's head, and Stasik was smearing it around on the desk and blowing with all his might, dusting all his neighbours. Oleg almost always did his homework and wanted to say yes, but Stasik hit him on the leg, painfully.

'I didn't do any!' Oleg yelled. 'I'll never do any!'

'But why?' Dasha asked.

Instead of answering, Oleg threw his hat into the air. It flopped down on to the teacher's desk, releasing a cloud of white dust.

Gaynulla lumbered into the room, opening the door with an armful of wood. He couldn't get to the stove and started pushing desks aside with his foot. Nobody gave him any help. The class started yelling again, even louder than before. Gaynulla dumped the billets at the stove and stood up, pulling down his tunic at the back. Silently he raised his arm, shook his wooden fist and froze.

Evidently, with her woman's intuition, Dasha had suddenly felt something. She blushed, turned away from the class and went to the blackboard to write something. The dust cloth flew across the room and, lightly grazing the teacher, smacked up against the blackboard. Dasha put down the chalk without finishing her phrase, turned towards the class and stood like someone on trial, slender, so pale as to be almost transparent. The class began to shout, whistle and ululate with renewed vigour. Then the teacher started to fight her way through the desks to the stove.

She went up to Gaynulla, still standing with his wooden fist raised, raised up on tiptoe and kissed his unshaven cheek. Instantly silence fell in the classroom. Dasha tripped the lever to lower his hand back down and said: 'Don't worry, I'll leave.'

Not paying attention to any of the pupils seated at their desks, she fought her way back to her teacher's desk, snatched up her small brief-case and, getting chalk all over herself, beat a firm retreat from the class by the same route. Gaynulla slowly shook his head in disbelief and opened his arms wide. He had become broader and more majestic with his prosthetic arm. With his arms wide, he walked out. Stasik immediately crawled on to his desk and celebrated the victory, waving his hands. But the stove remained unlit, and everyone sat shivering with the cold.

A period and a half before the long break Dasha Viktorovna hadn't returned. After the bell, before even the liveliest amongst them had managed to tear out of class, she came with the loaf of bread and the little bag of sugar. Hunger made everyone quietly take their seats and wait. Three dozen pairs of eyes attentively followed her every movement. The pupils sitting in the foremost rows were already breathing in the aroma of the warm rye bread.

The loaf crunched under the knife cutting off its heel. Now the smell of the fresh bread reached the rear desks. Oleg swallowed. Stasik, noticing it, looked at him in contempt.

'You sissy!' he muttered.

He jumped up on his desk and shouted at Dasha Viktorovna: 'You don't even have to try! We're not going to eat it anyway. Scoff it yourself!'

Dasha burst into tears but continued cutting off slices, and her tears fell on to the bread. Stasik looked around the class.

'You're all sissies!' he said. 'Sold yourselves for a hunk of bread. Well, to hell with all of you!'

Jumping back down to the floor, he climbed into his desk.

'I told my mother not to get married again or I'd leave,' he said, without addressing anyone in particular. 'And I will now.'

Stasik pulled his bag out of the desk, tore his jacket off the nail and slammed the door with such force that chunks of plaster fell from the ceiling. Leaving the loaf half sliced, Dasha ran out after him.

They threw themselves on the bread in a mob, tearing it into pieces any old way and started digging handfuls of sugar out of the bag, fighting over it. Half of it spilled out, the slices of bread were crumbled to pieces, and the crumbs were picked off the floor and hurriedly thrust into their mouths. Some of them wound up with a lot, others got nothing at all.

From behind Oleg came the sound of sobbing. Patrikeyeva lay on her desk, her shoulders shuddering. Oleg patted her on the shoulder.

'What's wrong, Patrikey-ha? Hey, what's up with you?'

'You're all creeps! Wha' creeps you people are! Scum!'

'And her?' Oleg asked. 'It's her own fault!'

'Wha' did she do that was so wrong? Wha'?'

'You know yourself!'

'I know, but do you?'

'Well, what, then? What do you know?'

'That Gaynulla is her brother. Her own brother. They're from our village and live next to me here. But you – you're creeps . . .'

She snatched up her pen from the desk and pulled her hand back to stab him with it. Oleg instinctively brought a hand up to cover his face and then cried out in pain. Silence fell on the classroom. Everyone gathered around them and looked at them, now at Nemets, now at Patrikeyeva.

The next morning a new teacher arrived. She told them her name, and it was as colourless as she herself was. From this point on almost everything had flown from Oleg's memory. He remembered only a sturdy woman with a hoarse male voice and a moustache sitting facing them. She had stopped teaching long before, but she had been called back to the district department of people's education. It was the war, after all, and everyone had their obligations. Her, too. Oleg remembered her moustache and – to put it more precisely – the cavalry-like commands that would come out whenever she got indignant.

'Get up! Sit down! Everyone march behind me! Tell your mother to show up!'

Stasik, who came back three days later, caught it from the new teacher more than anyone else. He irritated her.

Yes, what was destined had come to pass. The war wounded children, and the children wounded other people. Dasha Viktorovna never came back. Patrikeyeva said that she was working somewhere else and had decided not to come back to school. Gaynulla left to be caretaker at the neighbouring hospital . . .

The bus pulled up heavily at a stop. The elderly woman holding on to the railing with her narrow hands looked past Oleg down the bus and gave a tiny smile. Or maybe it just seemed that way to him: it was the mole on her cheek that was giving her an air of levity.

The doors opened with a screech. Oleg suddenly jumped out on to the ground before he had come to his own stop. Right away it was easier to breathe. Dasha Viktorovna didn't look back, and the bus carried her off.

Standing at the deserted crossroads, Oleg unclenched his fingers and raised his palm to his eyes. The ink-mark from the pen that Patrikeyeva had stuck into him sat there beside his thumb, blue, like a tattoo begun but never finished.

# SOMEONE ELSE'S WEDDING

The door was unlocked. Oleg's and Lyuska's mother opened it and saw that they were sitting in the half-darkness, wrapped up in a blanket. Completely numb with cold, the poor things. The stove was cold, but the firewood, sawn and split, lay beside it – that was their job.

'You must be hungry. Why didn't you light the stove, girl?'

'We've been waiting for you!'

'Then help me quick as you can. Almost like in the fairy-tale: your mother has come home and brought you some bones . . .'

Lyuska tore herself out from under the blanket and began to sort out the bones and wash them. Their mother meanwhile lit the stove and, in order to cheer up her children, said: 'That Marina got a letter again!'

'And didn't give it to you to read again?' asked Lyuska. 'And didn't read it herself, I'll bet! How stupid!'

'Didn't read it herself, but she did give it to me . . .'

'Let me have a look at it!'

'Wait, let's eat first . . .'

Their mother stirred the broth in the pot, while Oleg stood next to her, his mouth watering.

Making broth was a family ritual. Once a week their mother would bring some bones home. At the processing plant the meat had been painstakingly stripped off them for sausages; the sausages were sent, so they said, to the army, and the bones were given out to the employees of the meat plant where their mother worked as a typist. When steam appeared above the pot the children would breathe in the aroma with gusto. But making broth takes a while, and they had to wait in torment until the happy moment came when they could eat.

Their mother wasn't in a hurry to talk about the letter, chattering on about all sorts of nonsense instead. Then, concentrating, she skimmed the froth off the top and set it aside on a saucer. The froth would be for dessert.

Their meal's happy moment flew past in an instant, and for a while they felt full. After eating, Oleg and Lyuska climbed on to the bed and sat, coughing from the smoke in the room and warming each other, while their mother read them someone else's letter that she had brought home from work.

If she knew anything at all, their mother knew everything about letters. Along with her responsibilities as a typist, she had to sign for the mail. In the morning she would rush off to the head office so that she could sort out the correspondence herself. Business letters were put aside (they wouldn't go anywhere), while she delivered the personal ones. Some people would have made them go dance for their letters. But their mother couldn't stand jokes like that. She liked to hand over the letters as quickly as possible; she liked it but it did make her nervous at the same time.

Marina's letters were special. That is why they brought the Nemets family such vicarious joy. After all, their father hadn't written lately. Everyone considered Marina, a planner at the plant, to be a friend of their mother's, even though she was ten years younger. She rented a place not far from the plant. Marina, dark-complexioned and black-eyebrowed amongst the rest of the pale refugees, had been evacuated to the Urals from the Ukraine. Her nose and cheeks were freckled – just a little, just enough to look incredibly endearing.

'Oh, you're so lucky, Marina,' their mother used to say to her. 'Lord, what a beauty you are!'

'Don't be teasing me!' Marina would burst out laughing, as if she had never looked into a mirror.

A lot of men cruised around her, some of them with serious intent. But she wouldn't favour any of them with even the slightest of reassuring smiles. Whatever they said to her, whatever they proposed, she would just laugh, and that was it. If anyone was more impudent than that, then she would give the lout such a rebuff that for the rest of the day, say, he would feel like a boiled crayfish and the next day would think twice before trying something again.

There was a reason for her being proud and unapproachable: a soldier called Grisha was writing to her regularly, and she was writing back.

They had been going out together since schooldays in their little town, and then they had gone off together to study at the technical college in their provincial centre, from where Grisha had been conscripted on the first day of the war. As for Marina, she cried away her loneliness, remaining at the college hostel until the fascists reached the very outskirts of the town. Then she ran, following her nose, and by some miracle escaped.

No one at the plant received as many letters as Marina did. When she read them, putting her work aside, all the women would look at her, and she knew it. She would never fail first to shrug her shoulders. There you go, it meant, what a goose, writing all this nonsense. But this was just for show, pure coquetry. Gradually her cheeks would get pink, and the further she read the more pleasant it would get.

'Madman,' she would say in a languorous voice. 'To write things like that . . .'

But it was obvious that she liked those things. In response to questioning glances from the other women, she would silently hand over the little sheet of paper, covered with minute handwriting to fit as much as possible on to the page. The women would read the pages over and over again, warming themselves with someone else's passion, and then later would discuss the details amongst themselves at length.

'Marina, were you carrying on with him?' their mother would ask.

'What are you on about!' Marina would laugh. 'How could that be possible, before your wedding?! There wasn't even any place to do it: both the hostel and the city park were full of people day and night . . .'

'Well, did you kiss each other at least?'

'Kissed? Sure we did. I wouldn't say we didn't. But for the rest, we were putting it all off till the happy day. But, now . . .'

Here Marina would break off and turn melancholy, which didn't suit her at all.

Their mother would bring the letters home and read them aloud to her children – but, in fact, for herself as well. At first she skipped the bits about kissing, but then she started reading the whole thing. Lyuska learned the letters off by heart. She had turned fourteen, and Oleg was a year older as well.

Marina's Grisha, although he called himself a foot-slogger in his letters, wrote little about the war in detail. Not just because it was prohibited by the military censor but because, evidently, it wasn't interesting to him. Mostly he would go on about how they had lived before the war, about home and relatives, neighbours, teachers, his classmates' schoolboy tricks. Then he would describe Marina in detail, the way he remembered her: her hands, her eyes and brows, her shoulders, her hair. As if he weren't writing to her but keeping some sort of diary. These descriptions took the place of meetings in the flesh. Grisha would fantasize in the letters about how they would live after the war, too. They would throw a great wedding do, everyone would sing and dance, no one would recall the war. It should be forgotten, as if it had never been. If it wasn't forgotten, there couldn't be any happiness. The problem was how to forget it, when all around there was so much blood and mud that it would take an age to get free of it. Grisha fantasized about coming home to his parents' with his young wife Marina. They would plant apple trees around their little house, have a boy and a girl and would race each other across the meadow to the Kamyshovka brook.

Everyone had taken a look at Grisha's photograph, many times over. Close-cropped at the induction centre, moon-faced, and black-browed like Marina, with large sad eyes, he stood at attention and stared sternly into the lens, the way soldiers always look in their recruitment photographs.

After school Oleg would often drop in at his mother's office and type away with one finger. The people there knew Oleg, called him 'the wee German' in his absence but loved him: one of them gave him a pencil, another an empty paper-clip box. Boxes like that were good for keeping stamps in and the nuts and bolts that the boys unscrewed from wrecked tanks at the dump.

Oleg was afraid of only one person at the office – the chief accountant, Korabelov. And, true, he was a stern man. When her co-workers gathered around Marina to discuss her letters the chief accountant would come out from behind his glass enclosure, hung all over with planning schedules and 'socialist obligations', written promises to overfulfil something that had not yet even been fulfilled. Everyone would quickly fall silent and instantly disperse back to their places. Korabelov, small and sturdy, strode solemnly around in a black, unevenly faded suit with worn-out green oversleeves. The features of his face were uncommonly regular, and his appearance alone inspired trust. If the day was a sunny one, then in the light it would become evident that his face was all pock-marked, and the lenses of his glasses were as thick as the magnifying glasses that the boys used to burn dirty words on to the wood of fences. The chief accountant would raise his chin high, silently looking from behind his glasses at the women, taller than he was. Everyone was taller than he was.

He was half blind was Chief Accountant Korabelov. He would bring sheets of paper up close to his glasses and read haltingly. He would insert his key into the safe by touch. As far as his age and the rest of his health went, Korabelov would have been quite capable of serving on active duty in the army but for his eyes letting him down. The women at the office could understand and forgive everything in those days, since they were all without husbands. Rumours at the plant were that not long before the war his wife had died during childbirth, and it was since that time that he had become stern and gloomy. However, when in a good mood, the chief accountant could crack a joke and even laugh.

The chief accountant treated Marina differently from all the others, not making that kind of exception even for the office chief, a woman who wasn't young but who looked after herself. He would dryly address all the other workers, irrespective of age or position, by their first name and patronymic, but only to Marina would he say: 'Well, pretty woman of ours, bring me the plan report for the old last quarter!'

The women didn't take offence at the fact that only one of them had been appointed to the position of pretty woman. Hardly anyone was worried about that sort of thing in 1942. And, besides, Marina really was beyond any competition.

One day the chief accountant's younger brother, Levushka, came by to get him to go on a fishing trip. Levushka was about forty years old. He wasn't any taller than his elder brother and was going considerably bald – his head looked as though it was covered with chick down. Levushka's wife had drowned the last summer when they were out for a swim together, and there were rumours that they had had a row and Levushka had drowned her. But maybe this was just the clacking of evil tongues. One way or another both brothers were living the bachelor life, without a wife, together.

Korabelov had been called to the front office just at that moment, so Levushka took a seat near the women and told them something funny. They got animated and started combing their hair, stealthily passing around a hand mirror from one to the other.

Suddenly Marina came in. She had been sent by the chief accountant over to the processing building for a production report. She cast a glance at the younger Korabelov, sat down at her desk and stuck her head into her papers. Levushka blushed, taken aback, and began to speak awkwardly. As soon as the chief accountant returned, his younger brother hurriedly rushed up to him inside his glass enclosure.

The women pretended that they hadn't noticed anything. Levushka Korabelov was a respectable man. He worked as an engineer at Military Plant No. 79, where they produced aviation instruments, and that was why he had a right to an exemption, a release from front-line duty.

A week later everyone heard that the chief accountant's birthday was coming up, but that didn't interest anyone particularly. They were all discussing something else: out of the entire office he had invited only Marina. The women twigged right away, and some of them were unhappy about it. Not because they hadn't been invited, of course, but because it wasn't the chief accountant that Marina was going to see. And how could that be? After all, her fiancé was at the front!

Under pressure from the group, the office chief personally locked herself up with the chief accountant, within his glass enclosure, and on behalf of the administration and trade-union committee hinted that the situation was ticklish.

Korabelov the elder listened to her calmly, without interrupting and even nodding sometimes as a mark of agreement, and answered sincerely: 'I myself am, generally speaking, against this sort of thing . . . But it's just a birthday. I never invite anybody, but this time my brother's stumping up for it. How would I know, maybe there's nothing to it, maybe they have some kind of deal between them, eh? They're not children, after all . . . And, by the way, does the pretty woman herself get a say in this? Has anyone asked her?'

And it was true. Nobody had asked Marina about anything. It had been decided for her. On the other hand, why ask, if the whole meat-plant office knew about her private life, down to the smallest detail, from the descriptions in Grisha's letters?

After the birthday party Marina came back to work as if nothing had happened, and everyone forgot about the invitation. But two days later, when their mother put an envelope from Grisha at the front on her desk, Marina read the letter and put it away in her desk and then locked her desk, as everyone noticed.

From that day on nobody asked to see her letters, only looking on enviously as she hid them in her drawer. The letters came as frequently as before, but their mother, as a loyal friend, tried to hand them over to her on the sly, so that no one saw.

The wedding was set for a month later – Levushka couldn't wait. Marina invited the entire accounting staff. The event was rare for those days, if not entirely unique, and everyone, naturally, got worked up about it. If nobody had been invited, or if they had invited only a select few, there would have been less of a fuss in the office. But now something got going the likes of which had never been seen before.

Some women declared on the spot that they wouldn't go for love or money. Marina's faithfulness was their faithfulness, and her betrayal now became their betrayal. These women could understand and forgive everything but that.

'It's her own business,' the others would contradict. 'She's not Grisha's wife, and she has a right to fall out of love. And even if she was his wife, after all, isn't she a human being? Anything can happen in life – "a new husband is better than the first two", after all.'

'But Grisha's at the front!' the first lot would remind them, in indignation.

'But surely that wasn't love! What the hell – they just kissed . . .' 'And do you think that if he gets killed she's going to sit around all by herself?'

'But he's still alive!'

'Alive! And Levushka Korabelov isn't? He's somebody important. And, besides, what business is it of yours? At least now we'll get to eat our fill once in this war.'

'Go ahead and go, eat your fill, but we aren't going!'

Sensing the ill will directed at her, Marina fell silent, burying her head in her registers. Only the adding machine on her desk squeaked from time to time. But it was hard to put up with it by herself for long. After work she walked home with Oleg's mother.

'How come everyone's angry?' she complained. 'What did I do that was so bad? So, Grisha and I had a thing for each other. You can't tell your heart what to do, after all. And, besides, that was when we were kids – and with Levushka I've become a grown-up . . . Take this, by the way, hide it, so that Levushka won't find it in my bag.'

Marina handed over Grisha's photograph to their mother. Letting go of it, she burst into sobs.

Out of friendly duty, their mother stroked her head and said soothingly: 'Don't get all worked up, Marina! They'll get to you, they'll mess you around, and then they'll forget all about it. After all, women are all different: some of us have our own griefs, and some are just plain jealous of you. Do what your heart tells you to do.'

Their mother wasn't speaking with total sincerity when she said that. Lyuska and Oleg knew that she disapproved of Marina, too. Like everyone else, their mother was hoping that the wedding would fall through for some reason or other. But she was sorry for Marina as well. That's why she was trying to be kinder, justifying one side and the other.

No more letters from Grisha were arriving in those days. How things stood between them now, no one knew for sure. Marina wasn't sharing anything, even with her closest friend.

Probably Marina felt that Oleg's mother, too, was dissembling, and as a result she avoided her. The bride-to-be didn't have any time anyway: after work she would run to her fiancé's home and, together with the Korabelovs' mother, get things ready for the arrival of their guests. All the reserves of that well-to-do household went into the mix. From the countryside, on a cart, they brought in foodstuffs that had been held back by the Korabelovs' distant peasant relatives from government requisition. Three neighbours came by to help with the cooking and the frying and baking of pies.

On the morning three days before the wedding Oleg's mother, at first light as usual, ran down for the mail and sorted it. Private letters to the left, business letters to the right. A letter from Grisha caught her eye straight away. She wanted to take it and put it on Marina's desk but changed her mind. A letter from Grisha would be the last thing Marina needed now – not with Levushka around to read it! And, anyway, it would be better perhaps for her not to have any sort of correspondence with Grisha. She would disappear out of Grisha's life, and that would be it. Time would heal all wounds.

Right, what – not give this letter of Grisha's to her? Take that sin on to her own soul? But that was just as wrong, too. What right did she have to do that? And, besides, Marina had to write him the truth about what was what, otherwise he would continue writing to her about his love.

Running into Marina in the corridor, Oleg's mother called her aside into a dark corner, where no one could see, and handed over Grisha's missive.

'No!' Marina protested immediately, catching sight of the envelope from a distance and hiding her hands behind her back. 'I won't take it! No way! What was is over. I'm tired of living in a corner of some other woman's house. But to drag it out any longer – Levushka won't stand for it . . .'

In short, she asked their mother herself to write an excuse to Grisha for her and let him know not to address any more letters to Marina. Whatever way he took it, that would have to do.

This was the letter that their mother brought home to read that evening with Lyuska and Oleg. The three of them ate up their broth from the boiled bones, along with some bread, and then opened the envelope. As soon as their mother started reading, she got frightened.

Grisha wrote cheerfully that he had been wounded in the arm by a shell splinter in battle and that he had had to play dominos at a medical unit for a week or so. His arm was still bandaged up, but it would be of use again soon. And his commander had asked him what he wanted before he returned to his front-line unit: a medal for bravery or a three-day pass, not counting travel time, for a visit home? He, of course, chose home. But since his relatives were all in fascist-occupied territory (alive or not, nobody knew), he would try to catch a flight going back to Moscow as soon as he was released from the medical unit. From there, by train, he could get directly to his black-browed girl, the only person dear to him remaining on earth, and he was already counting the minutes. If she agreed, they would get married right away. Why delay, when everything between them was clear as could be?

'How great that he's coming!' Oleg said happily. 'Straight from the front lines!'

'You're such an idiot,' Lyuska observed and mimicked him: '"From the front lines!"' . . . Is it you that he's itching to get to?'

Their mother kept quiet, at a loss, looking for some way out for Marina.

'You'll have to write to him straightaway and tell him not to come here under any circumstances,' Lyuska suggested.

'But where? Where'll I write to? To the unit? – but he's not there. To the medical battalion? – he's checked out of there, too . . .'

So they couldn't come up with anything. Their mother hid the letter in a folder with 'File No. . . .' written on it that she had brought home from work. Letters were sacred things, she had always believed. She saved hers and read them aloud to herself sometimes.

The next day Marina dropped in at the Nemetses' place and asked Lyuska and her mother to help her with things for the wedding party. She had worked this out in order to guarantee that their mother would be at the wedding.

'But I don't have anyone to leave Oleg with!' she said, trying to make an excuse.

'Bring him along with you. Let him join the feast as well!'

'Of course, Mum!' Lyuska said. 'We have to help! I'll wash the dishes.'

'Better you should wash them at home,' her mother parried. 'I can't ever get you to do them.'

'Washing dishes at home,' answered Lyuska, 'is boring.'

'Did you hear that? She's ready to wash dishes if she can come to the wedding!'

'Mum, maybe we should tell Marina that Grisha is coming?' whispered Oleg.

'Shush, son. Why spoil her mood? Grisha's too late with his showing up. Oh, my, too late . . .'

The wedding party began at noon on Saturday. Marina whispered to Oleg's mother that she and Levushka had been to the registry office already the Friday night before and this morning had done the church ceremony. The Korabelovs' house was a substantial one, surrounded by a high gloomy fence. A feeble old mongrel dog lived in the yard. It wouldn't come out of its kennel, it couldn't bark, it would just snuffle and cough. The Korabelov brothers lived at home with their mother. Now Marina was moving in.

She was going to catch hell, the children's mother thought. Levushka, although he was forty, was still a mummy's boy, and the old lady was tough. Marina's mother-in-law had already checked how well she washed the floors, scrubbing the boards until they were white. She ordered her to call her 'Mother' and hand over all her money on payday.

The herd of guests arrived. People crammed themselves into the party. Whoever came late didn't find a seat at the table and had to drink and eat standing in the second row. The guests partied all night long, yelling out toasts every so often. Whenever by chance they all quieted down they could hear the dog's straining cough outside the window.

'Dear Lord,' Marina suddenly burst out, 'it's not even going let us sleep at night . . .'

'You're not going to be sleeping at night,' Korabelov senior said, edifyingly.

The guests burst out laughing. Very tipsy by now, Levushka got up from behind the table and took down his double-barrelled shotgun from its peg.

'That d-dog is b-bothering my w-wife,' he said, stammering slightly, to the instantly silent guests. 'It's not g-going to b-bother her any more.'

'You don't have to do that, Levushka,' Marina screeched. 'Please don't . . .'

'Shut up!' he cut in. 'I've already made up my mind.'

The door slammed, and immediately a gunshot rang out from outside the window.

'Dance! Let's dance!' the guests shouted.

The hoarse old wind-up phonograph started to play, and a tango floated out above the table:

> I'm so endlessly sa-a-a-a-ad
> That my dreams won't come tru-u-u-ue:
> It's my memories' pa-a-ain
> That makes me feel blue.

Oleg's mother washed the dishes in the kitchen, while he and Lyuska dried them. Their mother thought it was strange that no one from the accounting office had come, not even those who just wanted to eat their fill. Grisha hadn't shown up: obviously he must have had trouble with transport and hadn't made it. Thank God, that danger was past.

Late that night their mother took her sated and sleepy children home, but celebrations kept going full swing at the wedding party. On Sunday morning, before daybreak, as Marina had asked, their mother woke them both up so that they could go back to the Korabelovs' and finish washing the dishes. There was one advantage to this: the children could eat their fill again.

That night there had been a light frost. But as it got lighter the sky was nearly clear, the sun appeared from beneath the horizon, and the ice rime started to melt. It wasn't clear whether winter was setting in or autumn was getting ready to come back.

The Nemetses arrived at the Korabelovs' early on. They opened the gate and came to a halt in front of the kennel: the hound was lying inside the door to its house as if asleep, except for the bloodstain spread across the ground, frozen around its head. The house was still. Lyuska and her mother started to wash the dishes, but Oleg was bored hanging around the kitchen, so he slipped into the living-room.

The guests who hadn't left were asleep, some of them on pushed-together chairs, some in the corner on the carpet. Those who were sleeping uncomfortably woke up and wandered around the house aimlessly. Two of them came into the kitchen looking for shot glasses for a hair of the dog, clinking glasses and taking bites in turn from a single pickled cucumber.

Someone wound up the gramophone. Levushka came out of the bedroom, yawning, his mouth wide open, stretching his arms. The down on his head waved around.

The guests, still in their cups, spoke up all together: 'Well, hey, young man, how's the wife?'

'Come on! Tell us about it!'

'What's there to tell?' Levushka said, embarrassed.

'She must be stingy, to let him go so quickly . . .'

Old Lady Korabelov appeared and started stroking her son's back.

'You're way too soft, that's why she's stingy . . . It's all right, nothing to get worked up about! A woman has her rights, too . . .'

Oleg was bored by all this talk. He set off for the yard and in the entrance hall ran into Chief Accountant Korabelov.

'Don't run around getting underfoot, boy,' he said without any heat. Oleg had been afraid of him in vain.

In the yard by the barn was a gymnast's horizontal bar. Oleg hauled himself up on it, started swinging on it, then slipped off and smacked painfully on to the ice.

The gate slammed. A soldier appeared in the yard, looked timidly around and, straightening the buckle on the belt binding his overcoat tightly around his midriff, asked Oleg: 'Brother! The watch-lady at the plant showed me where the house was. Is this where Marina lives?'

Boards creaked on the porch. A half-asleep guest flopped out of the door, grabbed the railing, relieved himself and went back in.

The soldier adjusted his pack with his helmet hanging from it and repeated: 'Why don't you say something? Do you know Marina?'

Oleg was frozen to the spot, sitting on the ice, trying to figure out what to do. He didn't answer but rushed into the house, clambering over people on his way to the kitchen, and grabbed hold of his mother's apron. She understood at once.

'Dry the shot glasses, my dear girl. I'll be right back . . .'

His mother threw her shawl over her shoulders. But just then Marina entered the kitchen. There were dark spots under her eyes; her freckles had turned paler. She threw herself on to the older woman, pressing her cheek against her.

'Don't leave, please don't leave!' Marina burst into tears. 'I'm alone here, just a stranger to them!'

'There, there . . .' Their mother stroked her head. 'Calm down. What's done is done. There's no way back. It's all right; you'll get used to it. Levushka is an easy-going man.'

'I don't understand him, don't understand him at all!'

'You'll understand. You won't understand him right away, of course. There's no getting away from it now.'

Oleg was pulling on his mother's apron. She moved Marina to one side.

'Wait just a minute,' she said. 'I'm going to help my son.' And she marched off right behind Oleg, straight to the gate.

The soldier was squatting down, leaning against a pillar, looking at the dead dog. Their mother looked around to see if anyone could see them and quietly asked him: 'Grisha?'

He nodded.

'Come with me!'

'Isn't Marina here?'

'Come along with me, I tell you. Let's get out of here, quick as we can!'

Their mother's conversation with Grisha was short and to the point. He settled in with the Nemetses on the floor next to the stove.

The children sawed firewood with him and went out into the forest, knocking down the resinous fir-cones and collecting them in their sacks, riding the trams from one circuit to another. Grisha came to life on only one occasion, when one frosty day he tied skates – borrowed from the neighbours – on to his boots and skated all around the frozen millpond.

The evening before Grisha's departure their mother managed to get some bones from the meat plant by a ruse, made broth out of them and served Grisha bowl after bowl. On the day she begged off work from the chief accountant and ran home so that she could see Grisha off. He wasn't there: he had gone off to the local military command to sign out before setting off. But something had happened at home, their mother guessed straight away.

Lyuska was sulkily stalking around the room. Oleg lay on the bed, crying.

'What's been going on here?'

They both fell silent. Oleg's mother sat down by him on the bed.

'What's wrong with you, son? What's the matter with you?'

'Maybe you'll stop loving us and abandon us, too?' he yelled. 'Then go ahead and do it right now!'

'Where did you get that from?'

'Because I understand it all now!'

'What do you understand?' asked his mother. 'There's nobody on earth dearer to me than you two!'

'I understand everything! First you love somebody, then you cheat on them!'

'Stupid!' laughed Lyuska. 'You don't get the difference: children are one thing, but this is men and women. They're always with one person first and then with somebody else.'

'With somebody else? You mean, to hell with Grisha?'

'You're a blockhead,' Lyuska said.

'Maybe I am a blockhead, but your Marina's a traitor!'

Oleg sobbed for a long time. He wasn't crying for himself but for Grisha. His mother couldn't console him; she just scolded him: 'Grisha's coming now, and you all in tears. What kind of man are you?'

But obviously there had been a conversation between him and Grisha before now. Because when he came back from the military office he silently packed his things and said: 'Thank you for everything. Don't come and see me off, you don't have to.'

'Of course we'll come with you, Grisha,' their mother replied. 'I got off work specially for this.'

They got to the railway station on the tram. All this time Grisha had been holding back, but here, at the very end, his spirit failed him, and he kept saying: 'How could this be, eh? How?'

'That's the way it is, Grisha; that's life for you. You can't force love on someone.'

Their mother was repeating these cheap sentiments mechanically, but they were surely necessary, like any consolation.

'So it's my fault. But what did I do?'

'Marina's not having an easy time either,' their mother said. 'The women are demanding that the boss fire her from the plant. They don't want to work with her. Love is that sort of thing . . .'

Although what sort of thing love was their mother understood less and less herself. There were no nightingales singing for her later in her own life. She turned into an old woman living out her life in loneliness, taking care of three grandchildren on her own.

The Nemetses stood around outside the carriage with Grisha. The train jerked, the couplings screeching. Grisha hugged Oleg and then Lyuska. He was too embarrassed to hug their mother and said: 'Tell her that Grisha, he says, wishes her all the best.'

'I promise to tell her,' nodded their mother.

He climbed up into the heated freight car and sat down in the open doorway, waving to them. Oleg, Lyuska and their mother walked along the platform faster and faster, trying to keep up with the car. Suddenly Grisha untied his helmet from his pack and threw it to Oleg.

'Catch!'

The helmet clanged, rolling along the stones until Oleg grabbed it.

'Why give it to him?' their mother cried in alarm. 'You have to have it with you!'

'Casualty of the war!' Grisha yelled.

'Grisha – next time be sure to get married first and then fall in love, all right?' Oleg offered up.

'Sure thing!' Grisha smiled.

The train's whistle sounded, and it picked up speed.

Their mother stopped on the platform and hugged Lyuska, who had burst into tears for some reason. Oleg, waving the helmet, ran behind the train all the way to the water tower.

His mother didn't keep her promise. She never said anything to Marina. After the send-off the Nemetses waited for a letter from Grisha. His photograph, the one that Marina had given to their mother, Lyuska placed on the windowsill, next to their father's photograph.

The Nemetses waited and waited for a letter from him. But Grisha never wrote.

# THE USHERETTE'S CRIME

Lyuska Nemets ran lightly, almost skipping, to the blackboard, and the sniggers reached her ears before she had even uttered a word. From lack of vitamins maybe she hadn't grown much and had come to terms with never growing up. But she was maturing anyway.

Every day when there was no one else at home Lyuska would flirt with herself in front of a small mirror, arranging her hair differently out of distaste for the hairstyle of the day before. She had sewn a black skirt for herself from one of her mother's, with buttons and a slit up the side; now the girls were whispering that the skirt was too tight around her hips and that it was a disgrace to wear a skirt with such a long slit in it.

'You don't do your homework. What do you do instead?' her class teacher asked with a suspicious intonation in her voice. 'You're gone from school for whole weeks at a time!'

'So what? I'm going to find myself a job . . .'

'She just keeps on being *rude!*' the teacher burst out, her voice rising momentarily to a shout. 'You've gone too far this time, Miss Lazybones . . . How can we stand for this in the middle of a war?'

She spoke like shells going off: *boom, boom, boom* . . . Obviously it was no accident that the big-boned teacher was nicknamed 'The Bomb'.

Maybe it was just because spring had come, Lyuska's mother thought. Even if it was a wartime spring, it was spring, after all! That very kind that so much has been written about, and explained about, that it's awkward even to say another word on the subject.

Whichever way it happened, at the end of the third quarter, just before the holidays, Lyuska managed to get five fail grades, all 'twos'. Her mother had been called in to school on three occasions, but it hadn't done any good.

The assistant principal rang the trade school next door: 'Would it be impossible for you to take on an eighth-grader, a really nice girl but a poor student?' There was no new intake at all for the next year at the trade school. The only thing left to do was expel Lyuska Nemets for the edification of the others.

Lyuska hadn't told her mother that she had been expelled from school. The holidays were going fine – why should she go and upset her mother?

In the mornings, after finding some pretty picture in a pre-war magazine, Lyuska would arrange her hair in imitation of the styles in it and dance around in front of the mirror in a made-up dance in place of her gymnastics. Then she would clump downstairs from the landing, deliberately stamping her heels loudly to disturb the neighbours, and run to the cinema.

After buying the cheapest ticket available Lyuska would sit herself down in one of the expensive eighth-row seats. If anyone chased her off, she wouldn't get embarrassed but simply shift her seat. Sometimes she would watch the same film several days in a row.

She would come home for a bite to eat some time in the afternoon. She and her brother, the two of them, would heat up the soup that their mother had left for them. They would eat silently, both busy with their own thoughts: Oleg thinking about his stamps (which for lack of an album he was pasting into his new notebook), Lyuska with her thoughts of not having to go back to school after the holidays. After eating, Lyuska would immediately run off.

'Where are you going?' Oleg would ask sternly, guessing at what was afoot. Although he was younger he was the only man in the house after all.

'None of your business!' Lyuska would answer with a charming smile. Out of principle she wasn't about to accept his authority.

Their school had been crammed into an old log cabin, while the real school building on the neighbouring street had been turned into a military hospital. Lyuska would sneak into it through a side entrance.

It smelled of chlorine. Which ward would it be today? Yesterday it had been 16; that meant that today was 17, on the second floor.

She opened the door and heard their raised voices.

'The artiste has arrived!'

'Have a seat, little girl!'

'Here you go, eat up some pudding first!'

Lyuska would sit down on an empty bed and say: 'Well, here we are. Which one did I tell you last? *At Six O'Clock in the Evening After the War*? That means now it'll be *His Butler's Sister*. All right, it goes like this . . .'

And the film would begin. She would retell the film in character, sing the verses, dance and set the scenes for the action, nimbly jumping between the beds and the night-stands. Whenever the orderly would come in, forcing her way through the crowd at the door and declare it to be lights out or doctors' rounds, the whole ward would beg her: 'Shush, there, Auntie Nyusha, let her get to the end of the film!'

The orderly would sit down herself, listening and laughing, and then afterwards suddenly remember again. 'You've lost your minds! She doesn't even have a hospital smock on! So now, march right out of here!'

Lyuska would straighten her skirt and run off without saying good-bye.

'When are you coming again, artiste of ours?' would follow after her.

'Maybe tomorrow, but then, maybe never . . .'

What she liked more than anything was the way the men looked hungrily at her, and that was why she kept coming back. But her extreme youth kept anyone from forcing his attentions on her. And anyway the wards were for severely wounded men.

Once Lyuska almost said something about school to her mother. But she could imagine what her mother would do. She would push aside her plate and fall gloomily silent and would say after a while: 'Well, thank you indeed, my girl! That's how you thank me and your father for breaking our backs for you, your whole life . . .' And she would hide her face in her apron. Her mother was tired; there wasn't any reason to add to her troubles.

On the Monday after the long holiday Lyuska grabbed her school-bag as usual and set off, as if for school. She strolled around town until ten, when she began her first film séance of the day. She bought herself the cheapest ticket and sat down in the middle of the eighth row in her habitual spot. There were few spectators, mainly children from the second shift at school. And the film was very interesting.

She returned to the hospital in the afternoon, as usual. Oleg went to school in the second shift; he was busy with his own affairs, while Lyuska, after eating lunch in silence, ran off down the neighbouring street. Today was Ward 23 on the second floor.

'Our sweetheart's here!'

On Tuesday, to make things easier, she left her books on the shelf and set off with an empty schoolbag. Oleg didn't notice anything, and their mother even less. Lyuska had already spent the money their mother had given her and Oleg for the holidays. There was none left over, and you couldn't get into the theatre for free.

Lyuska looked in on her mother's friend Marina to see if she could borrow a rouble. Marina had formerly worked together with their mother at the meat plant but had transferred to commercial adminis-tration. Lyuska noticed right away that Marina's belly had started to swell and that her dress was getting tight at the waist. Marina stopped cranking her adding machine, straight away took three roubles out of her handbag and then noticed the change in Lyuska.

'Well, now, tell me what's going on! What's happening with you?'

She didn't know if it was worth telling Marina about it. But the tears welled out of her eyes all by themselves. And Marina was a smart and practical woman, anyway. She wouldn't give away anything to Lyuska's mother, that was certain. The adding machines in the office were all screeching away – no one would hear anything.

Marina wasn't surprised when she heard about Lyuska's expulsion from school. She hugged Lyuska to her, stroked her head and said soothingly: 'Poor little thing! You're fifteen already, after all, but still it's an awkward thing. Is there somebody you like?' Marina held Lyuska away from her and looked her over carefully from head to toe.

The girl shrugged her shoulders.

'Don't be shy! It all happens at your age. What are you borrowing the money for?'

'For the films.'

'You're not fed up yet? Films, films . . . You'll have to get a job, my dear. As for me, I was dreaming of going on to university, but I didn't even finish trade school.'

'It's all right for you, you're married!' Lyuska burst out.

'Don't be jealous. You have to wait hand and foot on a husband, night and day. A husband is like a horse: you have to feed him, water him, wash him, clean him, tidy up after him, and only then can the family wagon get going. You've got more than enough time left. If you find a job, then you'll never be stuck, you can even go ahead and finish school. That is, of course, if you get smart. If not, it'll do the way it is. Anyway, everything will become clearer after the war.'

'Oooooh, we still have to live that long!' Lyuska was repeating someone else's words.

'What would you like to do . . . ? Why don't you speak up? You think everything's just fun and games? Listen, my husband Levushka has a friend at the film distributor's. His name is Yepishkin, but he's a serious fellow. I'll ask Levushka to talk to him; maybe they'll fix you up . . . But now get out of here, I have a lot to do. Don't cry, it'll be all right. I'll talk to your mother myself so she won't be too hard on you. That's better than her finding out by accident. Right?'

Lyuska nodded, hid the three roubles in her brassiere and ran off.

Marina kept her word. She made her mother promise that she wouldn't go on about it. 'Just let Lyuska get a job. It'll be a great help to you.' On Wednesday Lyuska dropped in on Marina to ask for some more money. But she wouldn't let her have any more.

'I haven't any. My mother-in-law takes it all for the household accounts. But here's some news. Do you know the Aurora Cinema? Go in and tell them you're there to see the manager. Explain to him that Yepishkin sent you. You won't get it mixed up? They need an usherette.'

'Usherette?'

'And what did you expect to be, dear? Charlie Chaplin? Go on, go on! The job's a doddle. You check the tickets, and then you take it easy, go pick your nose . . .'

'Can you watch the films?'

'Only all day! If they don't take you on, then come back, and we'll think of something else.'

On Thursday the former eighth-grader walked around the Aurora to get a feel for the place. The theatre's walls were dilapidated; only the façade was painted blue. At the entrance, boys were cracking sunflower seeds and spitting out the shells. The ticket window faced the street, and the cashier dozed in it. The usherette let Lyuska in to see the manager and gazed at her with curiosity.

Lyuska knocked timidly at the door marked 'Cinema Manager'. No one answered, but she let herself in.

To judge by his appearance the manager was about forty years old. He was sitting at his desk in a brown suit with a tie. He didn't look up at Lyuska; he was talking on the phone. He talked for a long time, laughing, then finally looked askance at her.

Lyuska was wearing her homemade black skirt with the slit and a lace blouse that Marina had given to her because it had got too small for her. Lyuska had put on some make-up and trailed one curl under her eye, like in some magazine from before the war.

The manager put down the receiver. 'Well, what is it?'

Lyuska explained.

'Age?'

'Seventeen,' said Lyuska, adding a couple of years.

Young for a job like that, the manager estimated, wouldn't be imposing enough but all right in general. She could probably handle it.

And, besides, it was Yepishkin who had rung him – you could take that as an order.

They put Lyuska Nemets at the entrance. The elderly usherette Faina Semyonovna started by showing her how to check and tear the ticket stubs, and explained how people would steal in without tickets and how they sometimes forged dates and times. Faina Semyonovna herself had shown up at the Aurora only recently. She had started working there only after her husband had been hauled off to the front. But she was already quite at home there and, in comparison to Lyuska, felt like a big boss.

'If anything crops up, Lyuska,' she instructed, 'yell for a policeman, but don't leave your post. It's better to let just one lout in for free than a whole bunch: this is government money, you understand!'

Lyuska understood. She learned how to check and tear the ticket stubs quite fast, her hands only a flash. People would come barging past, especially just before the beginning of the show. No one cared about you, they just wanted to shove through as quickly as they could. Everyone was late, but there was just the one usherette. She was the boss, she gave the orders, and you couldn't argue with her.

'Go on in, quick, don't hang about!'

The spectators would obey, running into the hall.

'You've got the show times mixed up, citizen. You want the next one!'

And some burly fellow, guiltily mumbling excuses, would back out of the place. If they had got it into their heads to be disobedient, what could she have done, alone against the crowd? Better not even to think about it.

Her former classmates sometimes appeared amongst the film-goers. They would blink their eyes in surprise. Once The Bomb, Lyuska's class teacher, came to the theatre. She stopped, blocking the whole entrance with her huge torso, and declared: 'Well, what are you doing here, Nemets, standing there like a post? Go back to school, tell the assistant principal you're sorry . . .'

Lyuska only smiled.

'Did I forget anything at your principal's? I'm doing fine right here!'

The dusty summer came and then the autumn, with its rains, and Lyuska perforce came to mastery of her job. Now she wouldn't run off to the hospital every day but only when she worked the morning shift and less and less frequently on top of that. She would be so tired from standing in the one place the whole day long that she would retell her films to the ward sitting on a bed and didn't dance around any more like she used to. She knew even more films by heart, now, though.

There were few people at the daytime shows. The first-grade boys she would call over and let in without any tickets, on the sly. But whenever Oleg came by she would sternly command her brother to buy a ticket; let him know that Lyuska wasn't going to do him any special favours.

The manager wouldn't let her sit inside the hall but made her stand guard at the entrance, although he came late and left early. And as soon as the show started Lyuska would quickly shut the heavy bar across the door and make her way into the hall.

She would watch all the films one after another and never get bored. She had a small notebook with her. At the top of every page the film's name was written, with crosses underneath it. Every time she saw a film, it was another cross. One film Lyuska had seen seventeen times; another one twenty-four; some of them only nine times or seven. She knew all the actors both by face and name. Russian actors from before the war and newer ones and English ones and Americans. There wasn't an actor she wouldn't have recognized if she had met one on the street. But Russian actors had no conceivable business in her little town; American and English ones even less so.

Sometimes, walking past with his businesslike gait, the manager would order curtly: 'Come into my office!'

He would tell her to close the door, take a seat and ask her how she was getting used to her job and if she needed anything.

'Need what?' Lyuska would ask, wondering.

'Lots of things,' he would laugh. 'For instance, for speeding up your ticket-taking.'

He would scrutinize her attentively, as if trying to hypnotize her, but wouldn't let himself do anything. He told her to sweep out the lobby after each show, so that the enterprise would be exemplary, in case of an inspection. Once the manager opened a drawer in his desk and took out a sweet, something that Lyuska hadn't seen for ages.

'This is a reward for good work.'

He got up from behind his desk, went to his door and locked it with a key.

'That's not necessary,' Lyuska immediately cut in.

'Why not?' he said in surprise. 'We just have a kiss, and that's it . . .'

The manager put his hand on her shoulder, squeezing with his fingers and pulling her towards him. Lyuska tensed and pushed him away.

'Not half! First you let me out of here, and then you can have your kiss! Or I'll start screaming.'

'What a nervous thing you are!' he said. 'I was just joking . . .'

He even took to making jokes like that afterwards, only carefully, even courteously, perhaps. Or maybe he just wasn't in a hurry.

Once Lyuska was late for the beginning of the second shift. Faina had finished her shift and had gone. The manager was personally doing the tap-dance and checking ticket stubs until Lyuska showed up. She thought he was going to give her an earful, but he drew his index finger along her cheek and walked off.

Lyuska always remembered that day perfectly, because, checking tickets later on, she felt someone's gaze fixed on her. Usually the manager would come out of his office and watch her taking tickets and then disappear behind the door again. But now she looked around carefully – the manager wasn't in the foyer. There were a lot of people outside at the ticket booth, particularly children. When the show had begun and the ticket booth closed, and all the latecomers had run past, Lyuska was already sliding the bar across the door when she finally guessed.

Not far away from the entrance a soldier leaned on a single crutch. One of his legs was missing. A shock of tow-coloured hair stuck out over his forehead. He probably tried pushing it back, but it wouldn't stay. His ears stuck out like a calf's. He was in a quilted jacket over an undershirt and riding breeches – meaning that he had escaped from the hospital. The soldier leaned back against the theatre wall, clasping his crutch against him with his long arms, and stared fixedly at her. When Lyuska glanced back he turned away, as if studying the times of the shows in the window.

His face seemed familiar to Lyuska. He had been coming to the Aurora for a long time. What did he need, this one-legged man? Nothing more than to see the film, but he didn't have any money. *Everyone knows how badly you want to see a film when you haven't got the money for it.* Lyuska summoned him with her finger. The soldier turned away and quickly stumped off down the pavement. *The idiot! I wanted to do him a favour . . .*

Next day the soldier wasn't there, but a day later he was leaning on his crutch in the very same spot. She noticed him before the two o'clock show. But when Lyuska called him over he sped off again. He was nimble on his crutch.

There was something in this that she understood, but she gave a forced laugh and, shrugging her shoulders, pretended that it was beyond her. Men frequently forced their attentions on her, and she often heard words behind her back. But this fellow didn't need anything from her. He just looked at her, and that was that. He didn't even say anything to her. *You can look as much as you like, you're welcome.* But what was so special about her? There were all those flashy women walking around on the street. What a sight! Dressed to kill, despite the fact that it was wartime. Pick any one of those – this one for money, that one for free. How could Lyuska compare to them, in her worn-out and mended-a-dozen-times clothes?

Two days later the young soldier again loomed large on the street next to the ticket-booth window, examining the programme schedule. After letting in all the customers Lyuska broke away and stole silently up behind the soldier, so that he wouldn't do a flit, and grabbed his stick with one hand.

'Do you want to see the film? Tell me, do you want to? I'll let you in for free. Wait here.'

The boy shuddered, blushed and looked down at his dusty boot.

When the newsreel started the usherette looked behind her and beckoned to him. The calf blinked. She was skinny and small, while he was half a head taller than she was and two years older. She led him into the foyer and barred the door. She bustled in front of him into the cinema, while he stumped along after her, not falling a step behind.

The film that was showing was unbelievably popular, and the cinema was full of people. Lyuska sat the soldier down on her own chair then brought a stool for herself from the lobby. Judging by her notebook, she had already seen *Wait for Me* forty-two times, and now, watching it for the forty-third time, she smiled in advance at all the funny bits and, moving her lips slightly, pronounced every word in the film, the heroes and heroines obediently repeating them after her.

She could feel that the boy was looking at her and not the screen. Lyuska would look sideways at him, and the soldier would immediately turn away. Just before the end of the film, she ran to open the doors. The boy was the last to leave. He stopped.

'Bye!' she said.

He didn't answer and didn't move from the spot.

'By the way, my name is Lyuska.'

'I'm Nefyodov.'

'Goodbye, Nefyodov. By the way, tomorrow I'm on the first shift. The last show is at two o'clock.'

The young soldier nodded and stumped off. She didn't follow him with her eyes; she closed the heavy door behind him and slid the bar home.

Next day Nefyodov was there by two o'clock. And Lyuska showed him into the theatre. It was interesting to observe how he watched the film. At times he would freeze, at times a shy smile would roam over his lips, or, all of a sudden, his eyes would become frightened. She remembered what was going to happen next on the screen and would try to guess how he was going to react. She was showing him her film and was nervous about it.

He wasn't like anyone else, this Nefyodov. She didn't believe anyone else's words for one minute, but whatever he said, yes, she would believe it. He stayed silent the whole time, though. Only now and then he would forget about the film and look over at Lyuska until she would pretend to be irritated.

Her shift came to an end. Faina Semyonovna was checking tickets for the four o'clock show. Lyuska walked out with Nefyodov. At the entrance the manager touched her elbow.

'Come to my office,' he said quietly.

'What for?'

'We've got business to discuss.'

Lyuska's hand was on Nefyodov's stick, and the soldier squeezed her fingers. She freed her hand and ran off without saying anything to him.

When Lyuska walked past her Faina Semyonovna shook her head disapprovingly, her eyes on stalks. The manager let Lyuska into his office, lit a cigarette, elegantly blew out the smoke and said nothing. She was waiting, her arms crossed on her chest. He closed the door, grinning.

'Don't be afraid, I'm not going to lock it.'

'I'm not afraid.'

'Have you been doing this for a long time?'

'Doing what?' She failed to understand.

'Don't pretend. It doesn't bother me. You let people in and you pocket the money. You people are all the same.'

She didn't say anything.

'It's a good thing that you don't deny it. I saw it all. I was standing in the back and saw it.'

The manager got up from his desk and stamped from one corner of the office to the other, almost brushing Lyuska with his shoulder.

'So, I let him in,' she said. 'So what?'

'You're cheating the state, not me, Lyuska Nemets,' he dryly observed. 'You're cheating Comrade Stalin. And this with a recommendation from Yepishkin! And you sit inside the theatre, abandoning your post. I've told you about that more than once, haven't I? When are you going to share? You have to hand over half of it. It's not for me – it's for the distributor.'

'I didn't take any money!'

Lyuska had known from childhood how to keep from weeping. And although it didn't always work this time she didn't cry. It wouldn't have done any good.

'Sit down,' the manager ordered, suddenly coming to a decision. 'Sit in my chair.'

She obediently sat down in his armchair. There was room enough in it for another girl the same size she was. He came up from behind, stroked her cheek and then his hand slid to her breast. She jumped up, darting to one side.

'You mean, you don't want to work here? You're opposing your boss. Fine! So take a sheet of paper out of the right-hand drawer. Write! Write this down: "To the manager of the Aurora Cinema". Did you write that? Go on: "Statement. I request to be let go at my own wish". Right. Now . . . sign it. You can complain to the distributor, but I advise you not to.'

'Oh, yeah, sure. It's even better this way!'

Lyuska licked at her ink-stained finger, shrugged a shoulder and walked out without saying goodbye.

The pavement was slippery. She shrank away from the white flakes that were falling reluctantly on her. It was snowing for the first time that autumn. Nefyodov was patiently standing by the poster, leaning on his crutch, waiting for her.

'I've been sacked,' Lyuska said.

He took her hand, held it and said nothing. He would have liked to comfort her, to help her, but he didn't know how to do it. He wanted to take off his quilted jacket and cover her with it to keep off the snow, but he was too embarrassed.

'You know what?' Nefyodov said. 'Let's go to the hospital . . .'

'What for?'

'It's warm there.'

'What ward are you from, anyway?'

'I'm from number seven . . .'

'Number seven? I don't go there. I only go to see the seriously wounded, the ones who can't get up. But you're a convalescent . . .'

'Let's go to the hospital. I'll ask the head doctor – he'll take you on as an orderly. We'll be able to see each other all day.'

'What a strange one you are, Nefyodov!' she looked at him affectionately. 'If I become an orderly, whole platoons of fellows will be pestering me, and you'll have to watch.'

'Just let them try! I'll give them such a hard time with my crutch that they'll leave you alone straight away.'

'As if they don't have crutches of their own . . . Well, fine, it's time for me to get home. My mother will be going out of her mind.'

Lyuska wanted to be alone. She was shivering, either from the cold and damp or from tiredness.

'What about tomorrow?' he asked, looking at her with frightened eyes. 'Are you going to come tomorrow? You coming tomorrow?'

She shrugged her shoulders nearly imperceptibly and walked off.

The manager of the Aurora opened his window, pushed aside the curtain and breathed in the damp air. Two silhouettes drew his attention, and he recognized them at once. On the corner next to the theatre entrance his sacked usherette was parting company with her one-legged ticket-dodger.

# MR AND MRS NEFYODOV

At a certain point her mother began sizing Lyuska up more attentively. Lyuska could feel her mother's discontent with her. She wouldn't reprove her openly, of course, being cautious, knowing that her daughter would snap back. But at the same time her mother wasn't as affectionate as she had been. Oleg would have everything written on his face, but Lyuska was a complete mystery now. Her mother evidently wanted to find something out from her. Every now and then she wanted very much to ask about this or that, but she held back because Lyuska wouldn't say anything, and what was going on wasn't clear to her mother at all.

Lyuska had fallen in love, of course. What a laugh! Well, let's say that was it. Let's say that she really had fallen in love. Her mother, who had already run through a lot of things in her head – which is also understandable – wanted to warn her just in case, so she would say things as if in some neutral way: 'Watch out that you don't do something stupid, my girl!'

'What are you talking about, Mum? What a load of rubbish!'

Lyuska already knew in advance everything that her mother was going to say. What kind of advice could she possibly give her?

'Watch out, Lyuska, behave yourself. You're still not experienced: you know what people have become? The war has destroyed everything human, and only the animal comes out in people now. If anything happened, your father would never forgive me.'

For her mother, everything had been simple enough, but now . . . *But if you, my mother, consider that your daughter is acting stupidly, you should have been worrying about it earlier on. That train has already departed. What does it matter what crosses your mind? You have to think of your daughter as a grown-up now, even though you think of her as a toddler. Once she's a grown-up, she gets to have her own private secrets. And besides, war is war, but life passes, like sand through your fingers.*

Her mother wanted to see what he looked like. Just so she could size up right away how good or bad he was. What did she need to see him for, if her daughter herself still didn't understand what was going on? *You'll take it all too seriously, and then we'll get into a fight.* Her mother would definitely say right away: 'There you are! I saw what was going to happen! And it did!'

*Consequently, it's much easier if Mother doesn't know anything, since then she won't be able to foresee anything either.* First Lyuska was going to work things out herself. *You just go ahead and snooze in peace, dear Comrade Mother, you don't have to run outside twenty times a night to make sure I'm all right. And if you want to frazzle your nerves that way, go ahead, worry yourself sick if you think your daughter is feeble minded.*

It was clear to Lyuska, of course, why her mother was worried. Just recently she had come home in the evening and Oleg – what devil had got hold of his tongue? – had said:

'I know all about it! I saw you around the hospital! You were cuddling on a bench – with a one-legged guy!'

'So what, Nemets, shut up! It's none of your business!'

What was happening really was none of his, Oleg's, affair; even though he was her brother, he was the younger. Oleg took offence at this.

'You think I don't understand? I know myself that it's none of my business. I just saw you with that one-legged fellow, and that's all! What is he – your fiancé?'

'Don't call him "that one-legged fellow"! He has a name, by the way: it's Nefyodov.'

'Let him be Nefyodov. I don't care. And you don't have to be afraid, I won't tell mother anything.'

'I'm not afraid.'

'And don't be! Only . . . Mother thinks that it's somebody other than Nefyodov. She's afraid that it's Crosseyes who's after you.'

'What is she – nuts?'

'She's fine! Crosseyes came by our place – she saw him. She saw Crosseyes around our building, but there wasn't any Nefyodov.'

'I chased Crosseyes away right there and then. I told him not to let me clap eyes on him again.'

'You idiot! It doesn't matter what you told him . . . as if he's going to listen to you! Now I'm afraid to come home from school. There's a lot of those guys, and do you know what they get up to, down by the dam?'

The goings-on of Crosseyes' gang down by the dam were known to the whole town. Lyuska knew even more about it than Oleg, because Crosseyes had been bragging to her.

He had already started pestering Lyuska when she was working as an usherette in the cinema. Lyuska tried not to talk to him and wasn't very afraid of him at work: there were crowds of people around, in the evening a policeman stood watch, and the military patrol tried to while away their time in the cinema. But Crosseyes would bide his time until no one was around and come up to Lyuska and say stupid things about her charms. He would even try to get his hands on her. Lyuska would shout: 'Hey, hey! Take your hands off me!'

Here people with tickets would normally be filing past, and Crosseyes would disappear, except for his eyes probing her and his voice muttering something spitefully through clenched teeth.

It wasn't long before Lyuska was sacked from the film theatre.

Then, on one occasion, she was coming home from the hospital, where she had already been taken on as a temporary substitute orderly – without any wages, just meals. From a distance she could see Crosseyes' entire gang hanging out on the dam, by the kiosk with the 'Ice Cream' sign. They had wire hooks to hitch skating-rides behind passing carts down the frozen ruts. They would lie in wait for little boys and try to trip them up by hooking their felt boots. They would pull the fallen boy over to the rail, crowd around him and cut off his skates. If he resisted, they would beat him up, too – and they would sell the skates at the flea market. The child would cry, and Crosseyes' band would jeer at him.

Lyuska was running home quickly, out of breath, already not feeling the cold or noticing the darkness: fear alone remained. It would have been nice to avoid the gang, but there was no other way to go: there was only the one road across the dam. The snow crunched underfoot in the cold, as if in spite. Lyuska was hoping that they wouldn't notice her in the dark. But a little kid they called 'Miniature' – who always followed Crosseyes around like a shadow and served as his errand boy – kept him informed about everything.

Crosseyes had already sent his minion to Lyuska at the Aurora cinema. Miniature had run up to Lyuska and whispered: 'Crosseyes orders you, Lyuska, to go to the rear exit after work, there where the rubbish bin is and where he, Crosseyes, is going to be waiting for you in person. If you don't come, it's going to be bad news for you.'

At the time Lyuska had turned away from Miniature, not even favouring him with an answer.

Here at the dam, as soon as she caught sight of them, she straight away started to limp. She was thinking that if she limped they wouldn't recognize her in the dark, and they wouldn't hit on her: after all, who needs a limping crippled girl? She walked, hobbling with all her might, but it didn't work: far from it. Miniature was the first to spot her: he crossed the road right in front of her to make sure then ran straight back to Crosseyes with his important news. He got up on tiptoe and, in his ear, told him about Lyuska. Lyuska ran, limping on one foot, frightened to death.

Crosseyes cuffed Miniature on the head and immediately ran to head her off. Lyuska had nowhere to turn. She just stood there in dismay, not knowing where to go. He came up face to face and started looking her over.

'Weren't you coming to see me?' asked Crosseyes.

'No,' she answered, 'not you.'

'Lyuska, you're not doing right. Why are you pretending to be a crip? It don't suit you one bit. You'd better not be squeamish about me!'

'Why is that?'

'Because I've took a fancy to you. But you just run past me. What are you, scared of somebody?'

'Yes.'

'Don't be scared. As long as I'm on the street, nobody's going to touch you, except me, understand? Let's go. I'll parade you down as far as your place, so everyone can see you're my girl.'

'I'm not yours!'

'But you're going to be. I've got no girlfriend at the moment. There's a vacancy.'

He grabbed Lyuska around the waist, turned her around and pushed her to one side of the road. If her father had been with her right now, she was thinking, he would defend her, do something, wouldn't let her be treated like this. Lyuska, hoping to get away from Crosseyes, walked with quick steps, but he stamped along beside her, not falling behind a single step.

'You,' he said, 'Lyuska, what you so gloomy for? Hungry, maybe? Don't be embarrassed. Tomorrow come by the dam, and I'll set you up with some bread. The van from the bakery to the shop comes by at six. Hey, we have a little fun. We open up the back while it's moving and chuck out a few loaves.'

'And what if they catch you?'

'If they catch you, they give you a stretch. Hee-hee. Maybe we'll fight 'em off. We got knives – good steel. German steel, souvenirs. But if they catch us some day, it'll be free food for us. Come on by, babe, we'll give you some bread.'

'No,' said Lyuska, 'I won't come by.'

'You will,' said Crosseyes. 'There's no way out of it. You don't come tomorrow – you'll have only yourself to blame.'

He suddenly stamped a foot and burst out singing in a ringing pure voice:

> My dear one, and I am yours,
> Do what you want with me,

You want to, you can use me like a toy,
If you want, pass me to the boys!
Hey!


He accompanied Lyuska as far as her place, and there was her
mother, stepping off the porch straight towards them: she couldn't
stand it – she had set out to meet her daughter on the way home.
Crosseyes had moved off towards the fence, but her mother noticed
him anyway. She took Lyuska by the arm and led her home. Once at
home she didn't ask her about anything, only made up her bed.

Lyuska began to get very frightened. And not just for herself – for
her brother. Crosseyes wasn't the sort to give up easily. And Oleg had
to make his way home in the dark after his second shift at school.
Vacillating, Lyuska finally decided to go and meet him on his way
home.

Probably Miniature noticed her while she was on her way there.
On the way back from school Oleg stopped suddenly and indicated to
Lyuska with a nod of his head: 'There they are, the whole gang.
They're expecting us. What did you come to get me for anyway?'

As soon as they came level with them Oleg got pulled aside by the
sleeve. Lyuska shouted at them: 'Don't touch him, he's just a boy!'

'Nobody's touching him,' Crosseyes butted in and ordered, 'Let
him go!'

They took their hands off him. Crosseyes kicked Oleg and muttered through his clenched teeth: 'Get lost: I don't want to see you any
more. Hey, who am I talking to?'

Oleg wouldn't leave; he stood there, because Crosseyes wasn't letting Lyuska go, wasn't allowing her to pass, stood there with his arms
spread wide.

'You're staying with us, darling. Don't you get it?'

'Let me go!' She tried to break out of the tight ring surrounding
them.

Crosseyes reeked of bathtub vodka. He grabbed Lyuska by the

collar with both hands and jerked her overcoat with such force that the buttons all popped off. Crosseyes bared his teeth and suddenly threw himself on Lyuska. Knocking her down on to the snow, he pulled out his knife and, pressing the blade to her throat, started running his other hand over her. Those standing around chuckled, whistled, egged Crosseyes on. Lyuska twisted away, trying to protect now one part of her body, now another; she began to scream, but somebody ripped off her knitted cap and jammed it into her mouth. She pushed him away with all her might, and then his friends pulled her arms wide and held them down with their feet.

Oleg crawled between the legs of those in the circle and, grabbing Crosseyes by the leg, bit him. Crosseyes cursed vilely and kicked Oleg in the crotch with his boot, so that he rolled away and lay unconscious for some time, not even feeling it when the others kicked him.

Crosseyes did his worst to Lyuska, but she moaned and squirmed so much that the whole thing happened quickly and clumsily. And then he had half risen up, on his knees beside her legs; he had calmed down and now even pulled her cap out of her mouth and helped her to stand up. She sobbed and held the skirts of her overcoat down with her hands, although she wasn't cold. His friends had fallen silent, waiting to see what their chieftain was going to do next.

'Let her go,' he bellowed, buttoning his trousers.

Lyuska was shaking, and she could barely stand up.

'It's your own fault, idiot,' Crosseyes was softening now, and he felt like talking, or maybe making excuses. 'You want a loaf of bread? It's pretty fresh. Feed your bro and your mother, too . . .'

She didn't answer but hid her face with her hands. She just shook her head. The ring of his friends opened wide to let her go.

'That sure is odd,' he continued. 'She don't want no bread, did you catch that? You're much too snotty, but we'll whittle you down. Here's what: tomorrow at six o'clock you'll go to the Aurora. I want to go see a flick with you, got that? I won't scare you; you already knows me. But now beat it, love – your brother's getting lonely over there.'

Oleg was sitting in the snow and half crying, half bawling. His lip was split open.

'Are you alive?' She helped him get up.

Crosseyes looked at them and, spitting, added: 'So, Miniature, you see 'em home to their place, so nobody else messes with 'em by accident.'

Miniature obediently trailed along behind Lyuska and Oleg. They shuffled along in silence, not saying a word, and Miniature trotted behind them like an obedient dog. He followed them as far as their home and then ran off.

Lyuska looked at herself in the mirror: the track on her neck left by the knife was still bleeding a little. Lyuska decided not to say anything to her mother and not to see Nefyodov any more, since now she was thoroughly ruined. But it wasn't clear how she was going to keep on living. Lyuska's life had been taken away from her; she would have hanged herself now except that she didn't have the courage to do it.

In the morning, when her mother ran off to work, Oleg suddenly asked while getting ready for school: 'Are you going to tell Nefyodov how Crosseyes was pestering you?'

She was at a loss.

'Don't you dare go and complain to Nefyodov,' she answered. 'It's shameful. He's been wounded and has to go around on a crutch, and they've got knives! I don't want to see him at all!'

'You mean you're afraid for him?'

'Yes, I am!'

'You don't want to see him, but you're worried for him. You mean you're not afraid for yourself?'

'Yes, I'm scared, but . . .'

What 'but' was, she didn't know.

Oleg ran off to school, and when he returned Lyuska realized that her brother was being crafty.

'You know, Lyuska, you have to go to the Aurora this evening.'

'Not for the world!'

'You have to, and that's it! There's no way out. If you don't go, they'll catch you again later anyway and torture you. Go to the Aurora at six.'

'What did you do? Did you go to Nefyodov?'

'It's not important if I did or not,' her brother answered stolidly. 'But Nefyodov did say that you had to come.'

Oleg couldn't keep quiet about it for long, and Lyuska gradually drew it out of him: her brother had skipped two classes and run off to the hospital. They wouldn't let him in, but then from a distance, through a window, he spotted Nefyodov in one of the wards, called him out into the yard and there told him the whole story.

'Well, not everything,' Oleg corrected himself. 'You can tell him everything yourself, if you want . . .'

Lyuska also learned that Nefyodov was silent for a long time, after hearing Oleg out, then said that he would turn the affair over in his mind until evening, but, one way or another, at six o'clock sharp in the evening he would be at the picture theatre and that Lyuska shouldn't be late. Then Nefyodov added that Oleg shouldn't come at all, so as not to bother Crosseyes or get in his way. Otherwise he could ruin everything.

Lyuska sat at home the whole day long crying but by evening had come to terms with it and decided. Whatever happened, let it be: she would go anyway. Oleg was right, she couldn't avoid going. Otherwise, Nefyodov would be expecting her and she would be letting him down.

So that was how she persuaded herself: she finally made up her mind that she had to lay everything that had happened in front of Nefyodov and then say goodbye. She tried not to think about Crosseyes. She didn't even do anything special with her hair, to say nothing about putting make-up on her eyebrows and eyelashes, something that really suited her. She used hardly any of her mother's powder, and – needless to say – put on no lipstick. She only endeavoured to retouch, as her father would say, the scratches on her neck. She sewed new buttons on her coat, muffled herself up to her eyes in a woollen scarf, sighed heavily, and off she went.

Carefully approaching the cinema, Lyuska saw from a distance how Nefyodov in his quilted military jacket stood apart, not far from the ticket window. He was holding his crutch in one hand, his other hand hanging on to the iron railing – it was easier for him to stand on one leg that way. The railing had been put in place to keep people from jumping the queue for tickets. Nefyodov was standing and studying the times of the shows. Lyuska came up to him, and her eyes flooded with tears all by themselves. They looked at one another, only the iron railing separating them.

'What's this on you, Lyuska?' asked Nefyodov, and put his hand on her neck.

'Just . . .' She fluttered her wet eyelashes. 'Yesterday I . . . cut myself with a knife, while I was peeling some potatoes.'

'Right,' said Nefyodov. 'Don't cry, Lyuska, and don't be scared of anyone. I'm here with you.'

All Lyuska could do was smile involuntarily through her tears. Although she was smaller than he was, she was sturdier, and here he was telling her not to be afraid.

Now Crosseyes appeared. He stopped for a second, puffed twice on a cigarette, gave a drag to Miniature, who was following after him like a tail, and went straight up to Lyuska.

'Hello then,' he said, 'you came, darling? I never doubted it . . .'

Stretching his arm out, he went to grab Lyuska by the elbow. But he didn't succeed. Nefyodov had instantly clambered under the iron railing and raised his crutch between Lyuska and Crosseyes.

'Let's go, Lyuska,' he said sternly, ignoring Crosseyes. 'It's time for us to go in. We haven't got time to talk to passers-by or we'll be late. We've already got our tickets.'

Crosseyes pushed the crutch to one side, let go of Lyuska's arm, then squeezed the soldier's shoulder with his fingers and muttered into his ear: 'Listen, you, Red Army! Crawl away from here before I rip your guts out . . .'

But there were people all around, and the policeman who knew

Lyuska from when she had been working there was standing two steps away from them, bored, smiling at Lyuska. Nefyodov took her by the arm and, banging his crutch on the ice that was sprinkled with sand at the entrance to the cinema, pulled her away to the door. Crosseyes trudged along behind them, obviously thinking about where and how he was going to get the lame soldier out of his way. Lyuska was obediently walking along with Nefyodov, but she was scarcely breathing – she was even thinking that she should stop and let Nefyodov go in alone: after all, what Crosseyes was going to do to him was too horrible to imagine.

'*Four Hearts* is playing . . . I bet you've seen this one already,' Nefyodov was saying to her.

'I've seen all the films,' Lyuska answered modestly, barely moving her lips.

Nefyodov passed with her into the foyer, holding their tickets out to the usherette, Faina Semyonovna, while Lyuska greeted her. Crosseyes and Miniature rushed up behind them, but they didn't have any tickets. The usherette reacted immediately and sternly: 'Your ticket, citizen! You don't have one? Then where do you think you're going and with a child along with you, too?'

Crosseyes shoved a banknote at the usherette, but she pushed his hand aside: 'Go to the ticket window, if you please!'

This was because the manager was standing in front of his office and watching what was going on.

The theatre grew dark: the projectionist dimmed the lights slowly with the rheostat. Lyuska was hoping that the film would start right away and that Crosseyes wouldn't be able to find them in the darkened theatre. But they still hadn't got to their seats when she saw Crosseyes fighting his way through to them after getting his tickets. Nefyodov and Lyuska were stumping along on one crutch and three legs, while he, on his two sound ones, was coming after them. But they were already sidling down their row to their seats.

Lyuska helped Nefyodov sit down, taking his crutch as usual, but her heart had sunk to her shoes. The newsreel started. Hearty music rang out, and Soviet troops were shown taking Warsaw, the fascists in flight. Crosseyes was forcing his way down their row in the dark, getting as far as them, but there weren't any vacant seats around them. Miniature sat down in the aisle and watched the film.

Crosseyes panted, breathing heavily, and said to Nefyodov: 'Hey, you, Red Army! Here's my ticket, shithead, now you fuck off to my seat, and I'll sit here.'

Nefyodov tilted his head so that Crosseyes wasn't blocking the screen and answered coldly: 'Thank you, but I'm fine here. So off you go, mate, and take your seat, and don't go hiding the screen with your carcass.'

And he pushed Crosseyes aside with one hand. From further back the audience yelled at Crosseyes that he was blocking the screen, keeping them from seeing the capture of Warsaw.

In a fury Crosseyes shook off Nefyodov's hand and grabbed him by the front of his shirt. 'Are you deaf? Get the fuck out of here!'

There was foam on his lips, and curses were rolling off his tongue. Lyuska sat frozen to the spot, only squeezing Nefyodov's elbow in fear. Nefyodov took his crutch out of Lyuska's hand, put the elbow-rest under Crosseyes' chin and with a single jerk brought the crutch up so that Crosseyes' head snapped backwards. Crosseyes knocked away the crutch so hard that it flew into the aisle with a clatter, while he reached into the bosom of his jacket, a commando knife appearing in his hand.

'Nefyodov!' yelled Lyuska in despair. 'He's got a knife . . . ! knife . . . ! knife!'

At that moment, from the row in front of them, two men got up and twisted Crosseyes' arms up behind him, bending him back over the seats so hard that it was about to break him in half. From either side still more hands came up and grabbed Crosseyes' legs in a deathly grip, so that he couldn't even kick.

People yelled from the back: 'Disgraceful! Sit down, we can't see the film!'

They were answered from in front: 'Right away, right away, citizens, don't worry! One moment, and everything will be in order!'

'Miniature,' yelled out Crosseyes, 'blow! Get down to the dam and call the lads – they're beating us up!'

'Shut up!' roared someone's gloomy bass voice.

Crosseyes' choking was audible. Lyuska could see that they were carrying him out and he was disappearing into the darkness.

A few moments later the people who had carried Crosseyes away returned and sat down once more in front of Nefyodov and Lyuska. One of them stretched back his open hand and shook Nefyodov's.

Hearing the shouts, the usherette, Faina Semyonovna, had rushed into the theatre. The newsreel came to a halt, the light in the hall came on.

'What's going on here, citizens? What's the noise about?'

Three men in sailors' pea coats, with machine-guns – the military patrol – marched into the hall behind the usherette. Only now did Lyuska notice that in the cinema, both in front and around them, sat wounded men from the hospital, dressed any old how, as only wounded men can dress: some in greatcoats, some in quilted jackets, some just in pyjamas. And in such a deep frost!

The patrol marched down one aisle and returned back to the foyer along the other. Having made sure that everything was in order in the cinema, they went out behind the usherette.

The lights went down again, and instead of the newsreel they started to roll *Four Hearts*. For the first time in her life Lyuska didn't look at the screen and could see nothing but Nefyodov. She remembered the crutch, which had fallen in the aisle; she bent down and picked it up. She passed the crutch to her steadfast tin soldier, and somehow it happened that she wound up with her arm in his.

Nefyodov leaned towards her, pressed her hand against his downy cheek and kept silent but wouldn't let go of her hand, holding it against his cheek for the whole film. At the end, Lyuska said: 'Nefyodov! My hand is numb.'

125

The film was over, and a jolly song rang out in the theatre. The spectators got up out of their seats and moved down the aisles in the direction of the doors marked 'Exit'. Suddenly the traffic came to a standstill. In the little room between the doors a crowd had formed. Shouts could be heard, and then it got quiet. The crowd didn't move but stood in a semicircle, not daring to go any further towards the exit.

'What's going on up there? Let us through!'

'Keep moving, citizens, don't hold back everyone else!'

'Where we going to move to? There's a body there . . .'

'Where's a body?'

'Here it is, right here, at the exit . . .'

'So we have to call the police! Where's the police?'

Lyuska and Nefyodov pushed their way to the head of the crowd and moved someone's shoulders aside: on the floor, by the wall, the crumpled figure of a man was lying. His hands were tied behind his back, and his head was in an oilskin bag, tied around his neck with a rope. The figure didn't move and had evidently already suffocated long before. Lyuska immediately guessed what had happened: she didn't exclaim in surprise or make the slightest noise, she just pressed herself against Nefyodov's arm.

He looked calmly at the body, even indifferently, and said: 'Let's get out of here, Lyuska. There's nothing here that's of any interest to us.'

'Listen to me, Nefyodov!' whispered Lyuska right into his ear. 'Let's go to my place! I'll introduce you to my mum . . .'

The spectators started moving slowly to the exit, fearfully stepping around the body lying by the wall. Only the wounded men from the hospital pushed one another forward, making their way out of the cinema, and, blowing out smoke from their roll-ups, joked as if nothing had happened at all.

Half a year later, when the soldier Nefyodov became a student at the Pedagogical Institute, and Lyuska and he went one more time to the Aurora to a picture show, Lyuska suddenly whispered to him: 'Listen, Nefyodov: I want you to marry me . . .'

Lyuska Nemets really did become Lyuska Nefyodova, but it happened after the war and not right away. Then the Nefyodovs turned her mother into a grandmother, presenting her with two granddaughters as tow-headed as their one-legged father. But that's a completely different, separate story, and it's time to put a full stop to this one.

# GLOBE ON A STRING

Oleg Nemets didn't like knick-knacks. Over the years they had built up in multitudes in his apartment – souvenirs, statues, various little hanging things. When, once they had set off for America, leaving them all behind, Oleg thought it was going to be for ever. But now even in his two-storey house, where it would be difficult to state exactly the number of rooms because of an inadequate number of partitions, knick-knacks were once again appearing, and their numbers were increasing even faster than before.

His wife liked them, her hands everywhere, arranging little elephants, dogs and cats, little Buddhas, Mexican dragons, Hawaiian figures carved out of lava, to say nothing of Russian *objets*: clay animals and whistles, *matryoshkas*, tiny Tula samovars, Valday bells, Vologda wooden toys.

Whenever she and Oleg went anywhere, she would bring something back, since there are always more than enough of such things in any country. With her new exhibits in hand, Ninel would rearrange the whole collection anew. These souvenirs sat and stood in the Nemetses' house on shelves, on tables, on windowsills, behind glass in the sideboard, on the nightstands in the bedroom, in the bathrooms – everywhere the eye was affronted, enough to make him feel like getting rid of them on the sly. Oleg had even had a fight with her about it. A modern person has enough imagination to do without decorative junk, he tried to convince her. Whenever a discussion would start on this subject, he was ready to persuade anyone that the most comfortable of rooms is the one where the ceiling and walls have just been whitewashed and no one is going to bring in any furniture. The fewer the items of furniture, the more air – you can eat standing up and sleep on the floor.

Oleg would talk like this not just to seem clever and not because of any asceticism. He really didn't like unnecessary things. However, he did have one exception that made him vulnerable in a fight with his wife, and for that reason she would never take offence. She would point wordlessly at the sideboard.

Nemets kept a knick-knack there that he wasn't about to throw away. He had kept it with him all his life. He had carried it to school with him in his schoolbag. At the hostel of his conservatory it had lain in a box under his bed. He had taken it with him in his suitcase when he was leaving the country, and, when they were rooting through his things, the customs guards had turned the object this way and that in their hands, to find nothing hidden in it, and chucked it back into the suitcase. Now it was behind glass in his sideboard. Valyesha, his son, had tied a string to it long ago when he was still tiny and had hung it up.

From a distance the blue sphere was no bigger than a ping-pong ball. But get closer to it, and you could make out the continents, the oceans, Europe, Africa, both Americas, Australia. But it was best of all to examine the sphere with the aid of a magnifying glass – then cities would become visible, mountains, rivers. Here was our Europe and Asia, sewn together without a border. On the spot where North America was there was a small depression. In a word, it was a tiny globe. Spin it with your finger and it rotated on its string. You just had to know in which direction to spin it, so as not to offend old Copernicus.

The sphere would rotate, come to a halt, and here it would become evident that it was, after all, a peculiar globe. All the continents were outlined in bold black stripes, the rivers boldly marked, too. Moscow, Paris, London, Peking, Washington, Rio de Janeiro – all were designated by dots. But there was something missing, something that has to be on any map: there weren't any national borders. All the continents were painted in a single light-brown colour.

In one place, if you looked even closer, there was a dot in the region of the Ural mountains. Oleg had put that dot on himself. He had scratched it in with a fork as a memento when he brought the globe home. It was in 1944 . . .

After school, Oleg had boarded a tramcar – tossing his schoolbag into it through a window – with a group of children from his neighbourhood. They didn't buy any tickets, and in order that the lady driving the tram wouldn't see them they crouched down low on the rear platform of the car. The car rocked from side to side and up and down over the potholes in the road as if it wasn't travelling on rails at all. The windows were all boarded up, and only on the platform was it light, because the door was torn off. The boys sat on the tram's platform and pulled out the evening's trophies from their pockets: empty cartridges, pistol rounds, alarm lights from machinery. An open-air market was taking place.

'Two bullets for the lamp-bulb.'

'Ten empty cartridges for one live round.'

'Let me have a look first!'

'What for? Never seen a bullet?'

They would be bargaining away, but here the tram would hit a pothole, and the bullet together with the lamp-bulb and the empty cartridges would fly up into the air and fall down through the cracks in the floor.

They would ride to the last stop near the railway station. The tram would come to a final halt with a squeal. The railway line went further over a marsh and an abandoned quarry, overgrown with small stinging nettles, to the factory scrapheap. The dump extended along both sides of the railway spur leading into a dead end. Every day the train with its heavy crane in front would be driven to the end of the line. The kids would hide themselves behind the bushes and nettles and from there attentively follow what was being unloaded today, patiently waiting.

The crane, puffing, would swivel around, and two elderly rail workers in torn military tunics would pull the hook over to the nearest flatcar, on which a smashed German tank, brought from the front for melting down, would be piled. The workers would wind steel cables around the tank, then latch the hook on to them and run to one side. The hook would slide upward. The tank, swaying and trying to cling to the similarly smashed monsters alongside it, would rise up above the flatcar and be slowly lowered down on to the scrap heap.

After that the crane would take a break, panting out steam, while the shunt-engine would nasally whistle and back out of the spur. The empty flatcar would be unhooked, and another flatcar with crumpled-up armoured cars or cannons would be driven up to the crane. The railway workers would hook up this smaller stuff two at a time.

After unloading the train, the crane would be driven away from the spur, leaving behind white wisps of steam and a heap of black soot on the bushes. The crane never succeeded in disappearing entirely from view before the pirates would pour out of their ambush position. Chasing after one another, stumbling over the rails, jumping over naked automobile chassis and torn clumps of metal, the boys would run down hell-for-leather. The important thing was to be the first one to the tank: the first, while everything was still in one piece, before anything was unscrewed or tinkered with, while the most valuable things had still to be broken off.

On that day Oleg flew to the Tiger. He climbed on to the tank's turret, tried to raise the rusty hatch – no such luck. Where could he get the strength for that from his meagre diet? His friends got to him, started helping him. The four of them somehow managed to lift up the lid. Oleg grabbed hold of the edges of the opening and jumped down inside. Everything further down was familiar. Your feet found their way by themselves. You just had to make sure to latch on to the right thing with your hands. In a flash you were already sitting in the driver's seat, sprawling back in bliss and total silence. You were separated from the world by armour as thick as a board. In front of you the narrow viewing slit threw light on to the instrument panel. They were all there, in mint condition: you simply had to unscrew whatever you wanted. This was a war trophy – in other words, nobody's in particular. It was bound for the blast furnace anyway, to get melted down, to get burned up.

'Hey! Well, what's down there?' they shouted from up above. 'Are there any bulbs?'

'Yes!' answered Oleg, tilting his head back so that they could hear him better. 'Nobody has robbed this one yet! Definitely!'

Oleg, barely reaching the pedals, pressed them to the floor. He started the engine, yanked the accelerator handle up towards himself, drove off. The engine roared. Only it wasn't the engine, it was Oleg himself who was rumbling:

'R-r-r-r-r-r . . . Rummmm-bumm-bum! R-r-r-r-r . . .'

Oleg fell silent; it became quiet. And now his foot touched some object that rolled over the steel floor, clinking. Oleg leaned over to look – it was dark down there, nothing was visible. He tried to reach the fleeing object with his hand and painfully hit his temple on a sharp projection. He remembered only grabbing the thing he had been reaching for with his fingers, passing his other hand across his forehead, smearing a stream of warm blood and losing consciousness.

He came to on a bed in a spacious room that looked like a classroom. His bandaged head hurt: it was spinning, he felt unbelievably weak. Around him wounded soldiers sat and lay on beds. He raised a hand to his face – he was holding something tight in his fist. He opened his hand – in his palm was an absolutely minuscule globe. The blue oceans and the continents were all where they belonged. Oleg took the globe in two fingers, turning it around. Light was falling from the window on to the world that he held in his hand; on one side it was day, on the opposite, night – just like the teacher had explained it in school.

His fingers were weak and disobedient, and the sphere fell to the floor. Oleg turned in his bed so he could pick it up, and saw that the globe had split into two halves, right along the equator. Oleg hid both halves under his pillow and asked a wounded soldier who was lying in the next bed with a bandaged head, too: 'Where am I?'

'In hospital,' the soldier answered.

'What for?'

'How should I know? They say your friends dragged you in. They were saying that you cracked your head on something at the scrapheap and they pulled you out. At the railway station just then they were loading some wounded off the train on to a tram. So they picked you up along with the rest; they weren't going to ditch you, after all . . . You should thank God that you didn't trip over a mine or a shell that hadn't been defused yet. They wouldn't even have bothered to collect the pieces.'

The surgeon dropped in to the ward. He sat on Oleg's bed and said: 'Still alive? Well, now, let me see your eyes!'

Oleg opened his eyes as wide as he could.

'Feel like throwing up?'

'Nah . . .'

'If that's the case, then you shouldn't be occupying a place here! They've changed your bandages, so you march off home. You can have a lie-in there. I've got seriously wounded men from the ambulance train lying around in the corridors. But you – hey! – you've only had your forehead sewn up! Give him some supper and chase him out of here! Come back in three days, and I'll take the stitches out.'

His mother got an awful fright when she saw the bandage on her son's head. In the hospital they didn't stint on the bandages, and they had wound him a whole turban. Three days later they took Oleg's turban off. The scar coming out of his left temple was to remain with him for the rest of his life.

At first, Nemets was embarrassed and tried to cover up the scar with his hand, touching it now and again with his finger. But the scar gave something criminal to Oleg's face, and after the war strangers to the neighbourhood would give him a wide berth. Since scars on anyone meant a man of experience, you didn't pester him. When he was asked, he would answer modestly that he had got the scar in a tank. The habit of touching his forehead with one finger remained, and you got the impression that Oleg was trying to think of something when he laid a finger to his forehead.

With the years, he got so used to seeing his scar in the mirror that, if the reddish strip had ever disappeared one fine day, Nemets would have been as surprised as the famous character from Gogol who wasn't able to find his own nose. But he was left with a scar the rest of his life, and there was nothing to be done about it. His wife was given to kissing Oleg on the forehead in outbursts of affection, telling him that she was kissing a war hero.

The tiny globe travelled with Oleg from town to town after the war, and now it was hanging in a sideboard at the Nemetses' house in San Francisco. But Oleg never knew why or how the knick-knack wound up in a German Tiger tank – he could only make up different stories about it. The globe kept its geographic (and perhaps some other) secret and wasn't about to share it . . .

And now the symphony orchestra that paid Oleg Nemets a salary for being able to move his bow back and forth over the strings of his fiddle flew with its full complement to Vienna. In addition to Vienna, the American musicians had been contracted to play in Graz, Innsbruck, Linz, and – at the very end – Mozart's home town of Salzburg, at an international classical music festival. After the ovation in Vienna, the orchestra was transported from one town to another in two tourist coaches half loaded with crates and instrument cases. Oleg was getting pretty tired and dreamed of flying back home soon, but a long trip via the slippery pass between Linz and Salzburg was in store for them.

It was getting close to nightfall, and the orchestra risked going hungry if they arrived at their hotel too late. Around a hundred kilometres still remained before they got to Salzburg when the energetic first violin, Amy O'Connor, warned that if she weren't fed on the spot she wouldn't have enough strength the next day to play Mahler's First Symphony all the way to the end. The driver nodded, stepped on the brakes, drove off the autobahn and came to a halt in front of a small restaurant done up as a hunting lodge.

It turned out that they had stopped right at the border between

Austria and Germany. All around them the forest-clad Alps were visible in the moonlight, while underfoot there was carefully manicured green grass. A path paved with smooth stones led up to the house. In the middle of its lawn was a wooden house with a large porch and a veranda with toy-like bright red and blue tables and chairs. Up above, on the level of the second floor, was a balcony all around the house, and on it was a white banner with the legend *Zimmer frei* – an invitation to rent a room.

Inside the lodge it was spacious, quiet and comfortable: a high ceiling made of planks, couches in the corners spread with jolly checked cloth and bouquets of flowers on the tables. Oleg sat down on a couch with his back towards a wall to get a view of the place. Across from him, standing out vividly, was a bar with a counter and high stools. The walls of the room were hung with animal skins, ancient hunting bows, guns and daggers. Whether all this wealth had come down to the host from his ancestors or had been bought in an antique-weapons shop, it all looked a great deal like theatrical props. In a corner next to a window, an elderly woman was sitting at a table, slowly playing a game of solitaire.

The host, a sturdy old man of a little more than seventy by his appearance, grey-haired, lean, brisk, about to close the place up, hadn't expected such an influx of people. He was all attentiveness and smiled non-stop.

'*Bitte schön!* Welcome!' And, waving his arms like a ballerina, he thanked everyone right away for nothing: '*Danke schön!* Thank you very much!'

Realizing that they were Americans, the host switched effortlessly from German to English. And as soon as he learned that there was a Russian violinist amongst the American musicians he personally shook him by the hand and said in Russian: '*Dobro pozhaluvatt!*'

Of course, nobody except Oleg understood him. Their host spoke awful Russian but spoke it none the less.

'So where's the border here?' Oleg asked him in Russian.

'De borter?' their host laughed. 'De borter runss troo my bet in my betroom. I slip Austria, and my vife slips Chermany.'

His wife came down to give him a hand and light the candles. Their guests discussed the menu, taking into account their hunger and their American dietary habits, so foreign in Europe. Mugs of beer appeared on the table, and the lodge began to get noisy. The innkeeper hurried off to the kitchen to do the cooking.

Quaffing a dark beer, Nemets sat for a minute with his eyes closed, as if meditating. And when he opened them again, his breath was taken away. Right above him on the wall hung a huge branching set of deer antlers. By all appearances, the animal must have been enormous. Perhaps it had even wandered in the woods not far from there.

But it wasn't the antlers that had surprised Oleg. He couldn't believe his eyes and reached his arm up and touched it to make sure that he wasn't imagining things. From one of the antler prongs hung a globe on a thread, an exact copy of the sphere that he kept at home in his sideboard. Blue oceans, brown continents, heavily outlined. The globe was swinging in the draught from the opened door.

Soon the innkeeper appeared with a tray and began unloading plates of schnitzel, trout and salad. Putting each one down on the table he repeated: '*Bitte schön!* Please! *Bitte!*'

'What is that there?' Oleg asked in English, pointing his finger at the globe. The innkeeper's hand froze in mid air with a plate in it. But he answered Oleg in Russian: 'Dat?' he was embarrassed. 'Iss it boddering you? I vill take it avay at vonce! *Bitte!*'

'No, no, it's not bothering me at all. I just wanted to ask what it was.'

'Dis my daughter iss hanging up. He iss studying here in de eefening. My daughter studiess in school to be a nurse . . . '

'I probably didn't explain properly,' Nemets kept going. 'What is that object? What's it for?'

The innkeeper looked suspiciously at Oleg: was his guest joking or playing a trick on him? He took the string from the antler prong and handed the globe to Oleg.

'*Bitte!* Dis iss a pencil sharpener. An ordinary sharpener for de pencilss. My daughter can buy in any shop . . .'

Oleg took the globe in his hands. Like two peas from the same pod, it looked just like the one hanging in his home. Only on this one the continents were outlined not just in one colour but many different ones. Turning the globe in his hand, Oleg discovered an opening in place of Antarctica – a hole into the centre of the earth. His globe had no such opening for a pencil sharpener. Inside, a blade could be seen, set at an angle.

A pause ensued. The innkeeper nodded. He didn't know whether he should run and get the rest of the plates or if perhaps the Russian had another question. The globe was handed back to the innkeeper.

'*Danke schön,*' said Nemets, exhausting his supply of German, and slipped into near-native English. 'The fact is, I've got the same kind of globe at home . . .'

The innkeeper was most likely surprised by the naïveté of the Russian. But his face gave nothing away as he politely bowed his head.

'But without any sharpener!' added Oleg.

'Dey could come vidout a sharpener,' the Austrian agreed.

'The fact is,' Oleg continued, 'that I found mine fifty years ago in the Urals.'

'De Uralss? De Uralss iss de border uff Europe und Asia. All de children in Austrian shkoolss knows de Uralss.'

'I found it,' Oleg continued stubbornly, 'in a Tiger tank, a smashed-up German tank, do you see? How did that tiny globe get into the Tiger?'

The innkeeper, smiling, looked at Oleg, as if remembering something long forgotten. His brow furrowed, he wiped his eyes.

'What are you bothering him about, Nemets?' the orchestra members protested, not understanding any of the dialogue. 'We're all hungry, and you just . . .'

'Yeah, he's going to burn all our schnitzels!'

'Leave me alone!' Oleg flared up. 'Let me talk with this guy. This is more important than schnitzel.'

'Nothing in the world, Oleg,' said Amy O'Connor, 'can be more important than schnitzel.'

When the other guests started fussing, the innkeeper remembered his obligations and ran to the kitchen, bringing out the steaming dishes to the remaining diners. Demolishing his trout, Oleg looked up now and again at the branch of the deer antler hanging on the wall. The globe swung from side to side in the air currents.

The orchestra members grew full, finished their beers and started hurrying each other up. It was getting near midnight, it was still a long way to the hotel, and before tomorrow's afternoon concert they would have to take at least a nap, if not go to sleep. The innkeeper walked around handing back everyone's credit cards, cleared off the tables, and walked out to the porch to say goodbye to his guests.

'*Danke schön!*'

Smiling affably, he turned to Oleg, wanting to say something personal to him, but he didn't know if it would be interesting now.

'Come to Salzburg once more, always it vill be very happy! Dere will be more uff black beer, de special recipe!'

'Thank you.'

'Yes, und de pencil sharpener . . .' he stopped short.

'The globe?'

'Yes, de glope prezisely! Yourss iss not sharpener, just de glope. Some of de Reich uffitsers vas vearing dat kind uff glope. Adolf t'ought all de fife continents vill be hiss brown colour. All fife would be Reich, yes. Austria iss small country, ve are not on ziss glope, none uff us iss. Den ve all vass Reich, and who cared about Austria? Yes! Where, you say, you haff found it? In de smatched tank? Yes! I vass in the Cherman army, too. Unifersal contscription . . . No, I don't haff de glope, I vass a zoldtcher. Adolf only gafe de glopes to de uffitsers . . . Den I vass in captifity – dat's vhy I spik Russian. Zix yearss in Bologoye camp. De glope – de Reich, now iss pencil sharpener. Maybe de very same factory now makes dem, ha ha . . . ! And vass you alzo at de var?'

'No, no.' Oleg shook his head.

'O, *natürlich*! Of course! You vass young! Dis vass great good luck! De var didn't make any zense. Stalin vass alzo a goot Adolf. De whole glope might haff been a ret colour! Two maniacs playing chess! Ve vass chessmen, it vass us who vass killed. People died for brown or for ret colour, not for happiness . . . Gootbye! *Auf wiedersehen!'*

Oleg shook the innkeeper's hand and touched the scar on his forehead. It was still there.

The coaches carrying the orchestra set off, and everything around disappeared into the damp grey mist: Germany, Austria, the hunting lodge they had just left.

Nemets looked out of the window. His bus was crawling carefully down the winding road. Its yellow lights barely broke through the shrouds of mist. Oleg recalled the dam that he used come home across, through just such a fog, on foot, chilled to the bone, skating along on the wet snow. People are badly put together. They remember everything. Remember even things that should have been scattered to the winds long before.

# UP AND DOWN

'I'm *ter-r-ribly* sorry, but is this rock vacant?'

Oleg nodded and waved him down beside him.

The heavy-set young man in very dark glasses waved his hand to two pretty girls waiting for him up the hill. They walked down, carelessly nodding their heads to Oleg, stripping off their T-shirts, and their billboard-beauty buxom bodies in their bright swimsuits – with cut-outs in front all the way down to their belly-buttons and cut-outs up the side all the way from their hips to their armpits – really did bring something to their secluded beach. The girls put their things in the shade of the huge rock and parked themselves on top of it.

'We're something like half acquainted already,' the young man spoke up, stowing in the shade his flippers and transistor radio, from which poured some rhythmic melody. 'Half or a quarter. This is just a trifle. We probably met in some post office or café. As I recall it now, you were with some interesting woman of a very imported-looking appearance, just old enough, which really suited her – don't deny it!'

'That's my wife,' he babbled.

'Right. Then you've made out all right in life. But where is she now?'

'She got a bit sunburned and stayed behind at the hostel. My name is Oleg, Oleg Nemets.'

'Nemets – the German! Wonderful! But the way you talk doesn't sound German, it sounds American,' the young man chuckled. 'Right to a T, just like my Aunt Musya, who came back last week from Brighton Beach. Am I right?'

'It's possible,' Oleg grinned. 'I live in San Francisco.'

'There you go!' said the newcomer, satisfied with his acumen. 'And

I'm Borya, Borya from Odessa. I'm finishing up at the foreign languages department, and I can smell a foreign accent a mile away, even though I haven't yet made it to any promised land. I'm Borya, and these girls are seriously in love with me. They've been in love with me the whole week already.'

The girls barely perceptibly smiled. Evidently, they had grown used to Borya's garrulity over the week.

'What do you do, Oleg, if it's not a secret? Big business?'

'Not quite. I saw away at the fiddle.'

'Wow! A soloist, or . . . ?'

'No, no, I just play in the orchestra . . .'

'Are you staying here long?'

'For five days following our tour: my wife was overcome by nostalgia. She used to come here with her parents for holidays as a child. And I was here once as a little boy myself . . . Now here I am, warming my stiff back, since I haven't got anything else to do.'

Now they were lying flat, although on different rocks, the four of them face to face, forming a sort of crooked cross. These hot rocks were in the Crimea, at Snake Bay, not very far from Koktebel village, situated, according to the great writers Ilf and Petrov, on the shores of the Eks Sea. From time to time Oleg would chuck pebbles into the water without looking. Borya set a bag of plums down in front of himself.

'Eat some, Oleg, don't be shy. They've been thoroughly washed, and they'll slake your thirst . . .'

If you don't know already, Snake Bay is, to this very day, a place where a select crowd sunbathes and swims. You have to swim there or, if the sea is calm, clamber around to it on ledges up to your knees in water, feeling your way over the stones with your bare feet. But it's a nature reserve, and you're not supposed to go there at all. There are no watchmen, but, if one did appear, all you would have to do is slip a certain amount of money, a modest sum, into their hand and the forbidden would become the permissible.

There isn't any kind of attraction at Snake Bay, if you don't count hunting for pretty stones – chalcedony and cornelian. They have almost all been found and sold, however. Amongst its pleasures remain plums and, for some people, deep-cut swimsuits. In this quiet, miniature harbour, fenced off from the world by its perpendicular cliffs and the sea, it is pleasant to experience a temporary independence from the rest of mankind, spitting out plum stones.

It wasn't boring around Borya. A vivacious energy spilled out of his tanned, stocky figure, with its evident excess of cholesterol. He acted as if he was indifferent to everything, as if he had already got what he wanted out of life. But he did it in a jolly sort of way. He joked breezily, without either descending too deeply into vulgarity or rising to any subject that was too lofty. The number of Odessa jokes in his repertoire was inexhaustible. When it became unbearably hot he would put on his flippers, plop into the water and lazily swim in a rather fine breast-stroke, overtaking his girlfriends without any difficulty. Their squeals were enough to bring paternalistic thoughts to mind, making Borya feel magnanimous. Then he would once more stretch out like a seal on the rocks and, if he felt like saying something, would touch one of the girls lightly on the neck or arm completely by accident.

No one had noticed where the two puny boys of around fourteen had come from to get to the beach. They appeared alongside and stealthily looked at the girls, who were no more than three years older than they were. There was indeed something to look at. The boys exchanged a word or two from time to time but then suddenly started arguing. Slapping each other on the back, they both jumped up.

Now the two gamecocks would start fighting, thought Oleg. But one of them turned back, passing very close to the girls, staring right where he ought not to, then flattened himself against the wall of the cliff looming over the beach, not five paces from Oleg, and started feeling around for a handhold. Then he grabbed on to a ledge, hauled himself over it and started clambering up the cliff.

Borya and the girls had meanwhile crawled down from their rocks into the blue water, since it had become unbearably hot. They splashed around a bit in the caressing waves in the shallows, playing with the seaweed, swam around for a while and came back, sprinkling Oleg with cool drops of water. The girls lay down on their stones, and Borya looked them over like a bull seal surveying his harem.

Afraid of getting too hot, Oleg went for a swim as well and, coming ashore, lay down in his old place to get dry. He turned his head, and his eyes ran up the cliff, measuring its height. The boy had made it nearly fifteen metres from the ground. This was getting the attention of everyone in tiny Snake Bay. Everyone, with nothing else to do, was looking at the figure clambering up the vertical cliff.

Rummaging in his bag, Oleg pulled out a bottle of mineral water, some paper cups, chewing-gum and biscuits in a pretty package – everything that his wife had packed him – and offered them to his neighbours. The girls turned the packages over and looked interested but drank only the water. Oleg chewed on a plum and spat the stone out into the surf. Everyone kept their eyes on the boy. He was speedily and confidently clambering up the slope, latching on to ledges and bushes invisible from the ground, step by step getting higher and higher. It wasn't that difficult to climb upwards, thought Oleg. Your feet found their footholds by themselves. When you are climbing up, you can see the bottomless sky in front of you, and it's pleasant to over-come earthly gravity.

'Hey, look, look!' the girls gasped with delight when the boy sud-denly hung by his hands alone, shifting from one ledge to another.

It was obvious that it was for the sake of that exclamation and not at all because of the bet with his friend that the kid was climbing the cliff.

Oleg stood up, formed his hands into a megaphone and shouted: 'Hey!'

'Hey!' it echoed from higher up, in the ravine. 'Maybe you should quit before it's too late?'

'Late!' answered the echo.

The boy stubbornly shook his head and continued to look only upward.

'Wow, he's really chewing up the granite!' Borya commented. 'He wants to show you, ladies and gentlemen, how purposeful a real super-man has to be. But he isn't a superman. He's an ordinary lad . . . Personally, I'm heading off for another swim, it's getting far too hot. And how he's frying himself up on those scorching rocks doesn't even bear thinking about.'

Soon Borya came back out of the water, pulled off his flippers and flopped back down again on his hot-as-a-frying-pan rock.

Now it was a twenty-metre drop from the boy to the ground. How many feet would that be? Oleg stirred his brains with difficulty. He had grown used to a lot of things in America but not to their measurements. The twenty metres separating the boy from the ground was nothing in comparison with the hundreds of metres of cliff looming over the sea, but twenty metres beneath you, from there down, with only rocks below and the cliff a vertical drop, is altogether too much.

After he had reached a little ledge where a half-dried yellow flower was growing the boy's pride was evidently satisfied. He tore out the flower and threw it down to the girls.

'A cheap trick,' Borya commented. 'It's not even Women's Day today.'

One of the girls picked up the flower and sniffed it.

'There's no smell,' she said. 'Just dust and nothing else.'

'Blow him a kiss,' Borya went on. 'I just hope he doesn't get it into his head to parachute down from there with some kind of branch in his hand. I'll refrain from any further comment for now.'

Only now, after throwing down the flower, did the boy glance downwards to see the result. And when he did, he shrank into himself. He suddenly looked wretched. All his motions came to a halt, and only his eyes looked around as he clutched tensely with his hands and pressed his stomach against the steep wall; then he suddenly discovered a tiny platform to his left. Scraping slowly along against the cliff, he got to it and sat down sideways, bracing his feet against the narrow cornice.

Borya off-handedly chewed on plums, spitting the stones as far as possible in an effort to prove to the girls that the boy hadn't accomplished anything significant. The girls had been snatching the half-dried flower away from each other, then holding it listlessly for a while. Now they began to get nervous. They pressed their slim white fingers with their clumsily applied nail polish to their breasts and, stretching out their necks, looked up at the cliff, their moist lips half open. Borya didn't like it that the girls were getting too serious and forgetting about him.

'Behold the courageous hero, dear ones!' Borya intoned this in the accents of a holiday-camp counsellor, in order to allay the tension, and spat out yet another plum stone. 'Look upon this with the eyes of someone who will be proud of this youthful enthusiast for the rest of your lives. He is following in the footsteps of our Soviet hero-fathers, who never gave heed to anything they did. The child in question also thought with hindquarter-sight, which propelled him up the cliff. Now he has to think with forethought about getting down somehow. Now we'll find out if he has as much before as behind.'

The girls wouldn't smile. They seemed not to hear him. They continued to look upwards. Oleg refrained from any comment. He and Borya exchanged glances. What Borya had said was a bit hard, like any other honest truth. But Borya was older and more experienced, to say nothing of Oleg. Borya fell silent, while Oleg was thinking the same thing: he had already burned with such petty ambition, and the kid that was hanging there hadn't yet.

Everyone who had ever climbed the mountains here, at least even once, knew the tricks that Kara-Dag – the Black Mountain – could play on you. The vertical cliffs of the long-extinct volcano disappear into the sea, where they are covered over with seaweed and shellfish. The paths amongst the heaps of gigantic stones are few and well marked. It is preferable to go through these passages in a close-knit bunch, since the paths are also at times tracks of human wisdom: wherever there are no paths you had better not try clambering about, unless of course you have no intention of returning.

The cliffs of Kara-Dag seem unshakeable, almost eternal. But if you grab on to them hard, they sheer off in your hand. If, in an unlucky moment, a piece of stone that you have latched on to in some dangerous place comes away in your hand, you will turn into inert matter of the kind that forms the mountains, the desiccated trees and the dolphins cast up on the shore. Sometimes you have time to be sorry, and sometimes you don't.

Every year eight to ten such pseudo-alpinists and wannabe rock-climbers set off for home in soldered zinc coffins. This is called statistics. The youth in question, ascending to his shining summit, was destined to be amongst the statistics, most likely. In America, thought Oleg, there was a special rescue service for situations like this. But what did they have here?

Some people have been lifted to safety by border police helicopters, but that is a long story, especially now, in this slovenly and therefore lazy time for the border service, now that they haven't even got money for vodka, let alone aviation fuel. Anyway, they try to lift off the ones who have already made it to the top. Helicopters don't rescue people from the sides of cliffs: they might smash a rotor-blade, and a helicopter without a rotor-blade is like a toilet bowl on castors. So he would have to hang on the cliff for half a day or even more until the local authorities could find some rock-climbers. But even this prospect would take some time to realize. They would have to be talked into making a climb when it wasn't certain who was even going to pay for it. It would take hours while they hammered in their pitons, risking themselves in their effort to lower down the aforementioned amateur on a cable. Besides, were any rock-climbers at all to be found? They were probably all off trying to conquer Everest.

Oleg felt that the boy up there had already chased these thoughts around in his head. Most likely, he had long since given up wanting to strike poses any more. When absolutely nothing pleasant awaits you down below, you just don't feel like putting on an act. He had calculated the value of the flower pulled up and thrown down, and it remained only to regret bitterly what was done and gone. Of course he knew – he couldn't have avoided hearing those stories about people who had perished on Kara-Dag, but theory was conjoining with practice on a level too high above the world's sea level.

The boy was paralysed, his feet jammed into a small crevice. For some reason Oleg could feel that the fellow's heels, jammed against the cornice, were starting to sweat. The boy was looking down, not knowing what to do. Whatever he did would turn out badly.

'It's a pity the boy doesn't have wings,' said Borya gloomily, tired of keeping quiet. 'Too bad he's not a Daedalus or an Icarus at least. A set of wings right now would be just the thing for him. But, girls, maybe he is an angel, and he's going to grow some wings?'

Oleg felt out of sorts. It was an ugly state to be in, when, as when you're small, you cover your eyes with your hands, keep your head down, and whisper: 'I'm not here . . .'

He had been in a position like that once in his life. More than that, it seemed to Oleg that he had already been in the boy's place, had experienced that state. But, first of all, it had been a long time before and, secondly, it wasn't quite true.

A year before the war, Oleg had swum into Snake Bay from the neighbouring tiny bay, riding on his father's back. His mother had stayed behind, waiting for them on the other side of the cliff. His father was snorting like a walrus and splashing around desperately because it was hard for him to swim with Oleg on his back, although he would never have let on that that was so. Oleg, unaware of this, spurred his father on with his heels and yelled: 'Faster! Faster!'

His father was trying to persuade him to transfer over to the backs of any dolphins sticking their heads above water near by (in those days, before the war, they were still unafraid of people), but Oleg thought that his father was serious and was really afraid of it happening.

Later, Nemets senior lay in the sun like a landed fish, his arms flung wide. Oleg, of course, headed straight for the cliff and attempted to latch on to the treacherous rocks, these beckoning ledges, just the way the boy had.

The same way, but not exactly. Because his father had been there with him, dozing but alert. His father lay coddled by the hot sunbeams but then had suddenly leaped up, sensing the trouble that was coming. He ran to the cliff, stretched as high as he could and grabbed Oleg by the leg before the boy could take the very step after which climbing further up would have been easy and fast, without any way back.

The son had got angry with his father and sulked. The son was demonstrating heroism, and his father had jammed a spoke in his wheel. His son wanted to clamber up to the shining summit in his seven-league boots, to overcome fear, to attain his goal, but his parent had cheerlessly pulled him down by his heel. Oleg lay on his rock, offended, while his father intoned: 'If you're going to risk your life, son, you'd better know what for . . .'

At the time Oleg hadn't understood what his father was saying. And his father didn't bother explaining; he just flopped into the water and swam off. A year later he had gone off to the front, his life at risk, and had never returned. Well, he hadn't gone, he had been sent – after all, he hadn't had any choice in the matter, everyone was at risk in a total mobilization, so what's the difference? He wasn't any kind of hero, his father, he was a most ordinary victim of circumstance. He was shoved forward to a place from where it was obvious there would be no chance of returning. But the wartime meat-grinder ground up people for the sake of defending others, there was no escaping that fact anyway, so there was at least some justification for the risk.

Oleg had been half the size of the kid who was hanging on to the cliff now. What difference did that make, though? All the boys in the world are obliged to repeat all the mistakes in the world. All of them purposefully search as one for some place to make a mistake. This has happened in all times and epochs, for all people and under all systems, and it will never change. No one has ever been taught anything by someone else's experience – that's the nature and doom of youth.

'An unpleasant sight,' Oleg said to no one in particular.

'Maybe we should beat it?' Borya suggested. 'It's past time to get our snouts in the trough, and we still have to drag ourselves a long way back to town. Our comrade up there is a dead duck, they're getting his death certificate ready right now at the Registry Office, but we've got to get on with it. We'd make a poor cushion for the lad anyway. Did you notice: his friend, the quick-witted guy, has long since dodged out of harm's way. Why? Maybe he got bored or felt like dining? Nothing of the kind. It's so he doesn't have to be a witness. What the younger generation has learned to do well is to clear off in good time.'

'Help him, boys! How long do we have to sit here and worry?' the girls turned and looked questioningly at the men.

'Hmm. Zat iz a progrezzive idea,' Borya shifted to a Georgian accent, jumped up and struck a pose like an anchorman-acrobat and looked at Oleg: 'A ztrong-man act! You, freynd, untup uff mee. Ze gorls, zey take zeir places un you. Alley-oop! Then what? There we have six metres, while it's twenty and a bit up to the kid.'

He lay back down on the rock and continued: 'I've got a counter-proposition. I give up my penknife, and the girls cut their bathing suits into strips. They make a rope out of them. They throw him the rope so he can tie it to something and slide down on it. That will be a patriotic deed, Hollywood-style, and moreover an aesthetically beautiful spectacle. Oleg, you probably have a camera with you, being the only foreigner here, right?'

Oleg confessed to himself that this nice Borya from Odessa, with all his temporary cynicism, was almost right. Maybe they could struggle the five kilometres through the rocks to the village and there try to organize some help. But that would take three hours at a minimum. The boy wouldn't manage to stay on the narrow ledge that long without budging.

And up there he did seem rooted to the spot, though. There he sat, biting his lips, holding on with numb fingers to the remains of roots from under which, now and again, clods of dry dirt showered down on the people lying below. Now the entire beach was silent, looking at the boy. He felt their gaze, trying to summon up his willpower, and his despairing *'Why did I do it?'* came across to everyone eyeing him. Oleg understood him. After all, once you've got yourself into a fix like that, you have only yourself to rely on.

Finally the boy came to a decision. Rising up slightly, he grasped the ledge with both hands, then swung out and hung by his hands, lowering himself one stage down. His foot slipped off the ledge. His fingers trembling with tension, he clung to the rock. He convulsively moved his feet blindly along the cliff and finally felt another ledge. He didn't look down: there was nothing cheery below to look at.

The boy changed the position of his hands, took a small step and once again hung by his hands. If the rock sheered off now, it would be the end. In this was the entire cruel kindness of the Black Mountain – Kara-Dag: the cracks in the rocks, carved out by blowing winds and washing rains, are visible from above, but when you climb down they're hidden from your eyes. If the Black Mountain wants to, it supports you, if it doesn't – the rock gives way.

The beach was silent. Those who had been swimming came back out of the water and quietly lay down on the hot rocks. The boy crawled slowly downwards, sinking his head into his shoulders and freezing after every step. Mortal fear numbed his muscles, wouldn't let him continue his movement. For his preceding fourteen or so years the boy had been in the charge of many different people, and now he was isolated from all of them. Now he alone was the boss, completely in charge of his own life. Alone, with nobody else. In this rare case his death as well depended on him alone.

The girls had hunched up into little balls and, leaning back-to-back against each other, were craning their necks upwards, two fragile figures, laughable and helpless in their compassion.

'There is no God,' Borya suddenly pronounced. 'If He existed, He would have swung down and saved that idiot.'

His voice had stopped being ironic and was now gloomy.

The boy had crawled back half the way down, and now the most difficult part was in store for him. The cliff cut back inwards, and to get any further he would have to overcome gravity in another fashion: with inhuman strength he would have to get his legs up underneath the ledge. But he didn't have the strength left. From the tension, his tight-fitting bathing trunks had loosened up and his privates were exposed. The girls modestly averted their eyes but wouldn't leave the cliffside.

Borya had stopped chewing on the plums. The young Christ who had voluntarily crucified himself on the cliff was spoiling his appetite.

'Shall we try it? Maybe we can catch him?' Oleg couldn't hold back and marched up to the cliff, forgetting that he had to take care of his hands.

Borya shook his head negatively. It was as if he were glued to the shore. Oleg got up on the rock, trying to reach up and support the boy's heel with his palm.

The boy was slipping, writhing like a snake, clutching on to God-knows-what, because the cliff at that spot was absolutely smooth. His panting was audible.

Everyone was trying not to look, but their heads rose when the girls gave a terrified squeal. Four metres or so were left when he slipped off, after all. He fell, slightly grazing Oleg's shoulder, and softly smacked into the sand between two sharp rocks, barely avoiding breaking his legs.

The girls ran up to him, grabbing him under his arms. He shook free and stood up by himself. He walked off to one side and lay down on a large rock, hiding his dust-covered, blood-smeared stomach. The puppy was nearly safe and sound.

Sitting on their haunches, the girls let the air out of their cushions, transforming them into bags and, putting on their sandals, minced over to the cliff, around which they would have to wade to get out of that hellish Snake Bay. After they had disappeared from sight, Borya jumped up.

'What a bore! Well, easy does it! I'm *ter-r-ibly* sorry . . . I hope we'll see each other before you leave. I'd like to get your address: never can tell when I'll find myself in San Francisco . . .'

And he moved off to catch up with the girls who were in love with him. Passing the ragged rock-climber, Borya gave the individual a hefty whack on the back of the neck, and the boy raised his head in surprise. Switching on his transistor radio as he walked along, Borya turned up the jazz loud enough for his mother in the city of Odessa to hear.

Nemets decided that he would stew a little longer at the seaside. This was his last day at Koktebel.

The hero of the day was lying half alive on his rock. Just to give him some moral support, Oleg winked at the boy, and the latter, surprised, winked back. His arms hung down from the rock like noodles. The blood had dried on his fingernails.

# VLADAN

During rush hour it isn't easy to get to downtown San Francisco from the north side of the Bay. The Golden Gate Bridge is filled to bursting. Cars either inch along or don't move at all. Only a few of those sitting behind their wheels get nervous about it, but it's usually a question of life or death for Oleg Nemets. Just imagine a violinist stepping onstage in the middle of Liszt's Second Rhapsody and telling the conductor and the audience, 'Sorry, I got stuck in traffic,' and then starting into the piece from the middle of it.

Today there wasn't any concert. He and his wife were going to a friend's for dinner, not in the evening but at about four o'clock. The sun had already shifted to the ocean side. The day, however, was a Sunday, and everyone was going somewhere, and the traffic had jammed up earlier than usual. Ninel was looking at her watch now and again, since the whole gang of Russian émigrés were going to head off after the banquet to see the Russian circus that had recently arrived in California on tour. They had already booked their tickets over the phone, something that Oleg didn't have the slightest suspicion about.

'Other people get to live like human beings,' said Ninel, lowering her passenger-side sun visor with its mirror to put on her lipstick. 'They go see their friends regularly, or they go to concerts, say. Once in a hundred years we're actually going out, and when we get there it'll be all over bar the shouting. Here we sit, like idiots, looking at Alcatraz.'

This song had grown very old by now. Ninel wanted to socialize, to catch the occasional show, but her husband just wanted to lie on the sofa.

'Well, how are we going to go to concerts if that's my job?' Oleg despondently pronounced his repeated refrain. 'After all, people who work in banks don't go to the bank at night for their entertainment.'

'We don't need any bank. It's a problem getting you out anywhere at all!'

'But at this very moment we're heading in to see our friends.'

'Sure, so we get out – once in a blue moon! And only because Miron is a close friend of yours. You couldn't turn him down . . . Can you believe he passed that crazy examination of his?'

'Only twenty years, and he's a doctor again. That's the émigré's life for you.'

Suddenly the line of cars moved. Off to their right they could see that a police car had pushed a broken-down pickup truck to the side of the road. Oleg stepped on the accelerator, and their Buick dodged around the serpentine of Presidio Park. It wasn't far now.

Miron Olshansky's house was new: front room, family room and kitchen on the first floor, without any partitions. Which is great for a huge get-together of eighty people, by the way, since the entire Russian middle class of San Francisco, mostly doctors, had assembled there. The party was in full swing. The people who crowded in, mostly unknown to Oleg but evidently well known to one another, were wandering around the house with glasses and mugs, every now and then pumping themselves beer out of a keg.

'We'll both take gin and tonics,' said Ninel, kissing someone.

'Show us the latest one of you to have become an American doctor at last!' Oleg shouted with a laugh.

But Miron, an old friend of his from Russian days, was already rushing towards him.

'At the eighth try!' he said beaming and shook Nemets's hand for a long time.

'Congratulations!' Oleg slapped Miron on the shoulder. 'Look at how great this is: I'm going to get kicked out on a pension soon, and you're a young doctor!'

'I've swapped for it: I got my second licence in exchange for the first loss of my hair.' Miron turned to his guests, shoving Oleg from behind. 'Ladies and gentlemen, I've invited a violinist for you, for a change, since you're all harping on about medicine here.'

'A fiddler? Where's his violin, then?'

'Can't you see he's got his wife with him? And she's the one he fiddles.'

'Is there going to be a concert?'

'Have him play the Soviet anthem in honour of our host or any other sort of requiem . . .'

Oleg was squeezed between two attractive ladies of indeterminate age, as they say these days. Without asking Oleg, they started filling up his glass and plate. Miron steered Ninel to the other end of the table, which was groaning under the weight of tasty goodies, and she was faced with the difficult task of deciding what not to eat.

Meanwhile, Miron, blissful from victory, guests and alcohol, continuing his mysterious pre-Nemets conversation, yelled: 'Quiet! You're all biased here, especially all you former Soviet urologists, and by definition you can't be objective. Let's ask someone neutral. Tell us, Oleg: which organ is most important to a man?'

Everyone at the table stopped rattling their forks and narrowed their eyes ironically at Nemets. Oleg didn't even think for a moment.

'The hands,' he said immediately.

'Why the hands?' someone asked in disappointment or maybe contempt.

'Don't listen to him. He *is* a violinist, after all!'

'A violinist? That means that he's been sawing away his whole life and still hasn't sawn through anything. It looks like nothing good comes of his hands.'

Oleg knew that to say 'hands' in the present company was a big political mistake: the urologists lost interest in him straight away. Oleg had done it for two reasons. First of all, he had decided to avoid saying what they wanted to hear out of a sense of contrariness, and, secondly, he really was certain that hands were more important to a man than his head, to say nothing of other parts.

'We're all narrow specialists here.' Their host put an end to the discussion and looked at Nemets. 'For all our liking for music, and for the fact that it's more suitable to play the piano or violin with two hands, we know better which organ is more important to a man. Let's drink to the prostate gland!' And he up-ended his shot glass into his mouth.

'Don't drink too much, boys, we still have to go and be entertained.'

'Where to?' asked Oleg in alarm, glancing sharply at his wife.

'Now, Oleg, dear,' babbled Ninel, 'I completely forgot to tell you: everyone has bought tickets to the circus. Once in a blue moon now the Russian circus tours around the sticks here in California. Just for old times' sake, come on, please!'

'Where is it?'

'In Oakland, half an hour from here.'

Meanwhile, the guests, looking at their watches, had started going out singly and in groups, plumping themselves into their cars. Those who had drunk too much handed over the wheel dutifully to their wives and climbed into the back seat for a snooze. Those who didn't know the way jockeyed to trail behind those who did. If there was a traffic jam at the Bay Bridge just then, it happened only because fifty-odd cars belonging to the same party were sticking close to one another on the highway to Oakland.

There, near the park, a crowd of people was already moving on foot and bicycle to the field, partitioned off with a temporary fence. Poorer people were trying to park their cars further away, so they wouldn't have to pay for parking. Well-to-do people, such as Doctor-Recruit Olshansky's guests, drove on to the expensive parking near the circus. There were many blacks amongst the crowd, since the circus had set up in their neighbourhood, and, it goes without saying, a lot of children. The place smelled of seaweed, creosote and spices from the neighbouring restaurants. In the centre of the field the tent rose, stretched in various directions by its cables. Air conditioners howled, pumping cold air in under the tent. They were selling tickets from a wagon.

Under the tent rumbled a kind of music that was hard for Oleg's ears to take, harmful even. He hadn't been to the circus for probably a quarter of a century and was frankly bored, lazily allowing his eyes to wander from side to side. The simpler sort of people, in the absolute majority all around, were gorging on the spectacle, on popcorn and ice cream, washing it all down with Coca-Cola and beer. Any American audience, as is well known, is full of *joie de vivre* and benevolence, and this one's appreciation of the Russian circus was no exception. Now and again the audience burst into applause, even if nothing extraordinary was going on in the ring.

After the opening parade, then the acrobats, the performing dogs, the magician who capably sawed in half his assistant in miniskirt and maxi-décolleté, after they pulled a boneless woman out of a *matryoshka* doll, who then performed intricate contortions on a gleaming sphere rotating in mid-air, the ringmaster raised his arms to the sky and announced the programme's next act: 'And now, ladies and gentlemen, before your very eyes – Vladan!'

Oleg, who had been listening with only half an ear before this, shook his head to banish his drowsiness, since he was certain that he had misheard the name. A tango struck up whose melody had all but departed his memory, but not entirely as it turned out. A spasm caught at Nemets's throat. He began greedily gulping down oxygen, as if the air had been pumped out of the circus tent.

'Say his name again,' he whispered to his wife.

'I think it was Vladan – why?'

'Vladan?!' Oleg breathed out.

'Are you all right?' Ninel asked in alarm. 'Is your heart acting up again? I'll find a pill right now.'

Oleg put the pill under his tongue, but it didn't help. He covered his ears with his palms and time condensed. Events in his memory twitched and flashed past in the tiniest detail, swirling – Nemets could scarcely follow what was going on in the ring. Moreover, he was seeing exactly what he had once before experienced half a century ago. As if his entire subsequent life had shunted to one side and nothing was left but his childhood . . .

Bright posters had suddenly blossomed in the dim and muddy spring of the war year of 1944 in his gloomy Urals town, posters towards which, sliding on the wet ice, the locals had rushed, unspoilt by any such events. Mouths open, they scrutinized the handsome and beautiful performers pasted all over their fences. The locals had quickly detached the pieces of the bills that appealed to them, but soon new posters were stuck up in their places.

On one of the bills was a moustachioed magician dressed all in blue with a black blindfold over his eyes, standing bravely in a fiery hoop. Beside him was a woman in a snow-white ball gown, like someone who had just stepped out of the pages of an old novel, holding a hat in her hands; a fluffy puppy looked out of the hat. On another poster were several infuriated tigers, licking their chops and looking at their beauteous trainer. One tiger held her head in his jaws, and the beauty was smiling with all her might. On a third one was a man in a black cape, looking like one of the Three Musketeers, coming down from the sky on a magic carpet.

*EVERY DAY*

was written in red letters at the top of this poster. While on the bottom were six bold black letters with three exclamation marks:

*VLADAN!!!*

The word lodged in their minds and all of a sudden became the most indispensable in town.

'Vlada-a-an!' shouted children out of doors, running around in the market-place.

'Vlada-a-a-an!' howled schoolchildren during break.

And nobody could explain exactly what this 'Vladan' was. People would shrug their shoulders, since any circus performances were as yet unmounted.

Just at this time a new pupil had been settled in at Oleg Nemets's desk. He listened to what the whole class was yelling but he himself just smiled. Their strict, moustachioed teacher wrote down his name in the class register, and then she repeated his name loudly a couple of times to commit it to memory: 'Akhmet Akhmetzhanov. Akhmet Akhmetzhanov . . . You're from the circus, aren't you?'

Akhmet nodded. The class started buzzing.

'Quiet, children!' their teacher shouted. 'This is nothing special! He'll be in class temporarily, until the circus leaves town.'

Oleg moved his notebook slightly towards Akhmet, offering him a landmine fragment on it. 'Take it! Take it for keeps!'

The new pupil had no interest in the thing. It soon came out that he had more important business. After school, Oleg and Akhmet went out together and stopped in front of a poster.

### THREE – AKHMETZHANOVS – THREE

– the posters announced, and explained further down:

### TIGHTROPE BALANCING ACT

The Akhmetzhanovs' father walked along a tightrope, holding a long pole – or 'balance', as Akhmet put it – horizontally. On Mr Akhmetzhanov's shoulders stood Mrs Akhmetzhanova, that is, Akhmet's mother. On her shoulders stood a boy – Oleg's new friend, Akhmet, who was enrolled, as eldest son, in the circus troupe of the Akhmetzhanovs. Two younger brothers of his, the twins Suren and Bulat, were also tumblers in the ring but were permitted on the high wire only at rehearsals.

'And are you going to perform as a fivesome?' asked Oleg.

'We've already been rehearsing for a long time, but we still have sticky moments . . .'

So Nemets was sitting at the same desk with a living artiste, and everybody was jealous. He soon knew absolutely everything about Akhmet. How he used to live in an orphanage in Tashkent and how Akhmetzhanov senior had adopted him. He and his wife had found all three of their children in orphanages.

And how much Akhmet was able to get away with! Nemets couldn't utter a single word without getting a reprimand from the teacher. But his neighbour could chatter away in a way that the teacher couldn't hear. Akhmet even taught Oleg how to talk almost without moving his lips. That was how the Akhmetzhanovs talked to each other in the ring, unbeknownst to the audience.

'Do you want to come to the circus tonight?' the new lad asked, when they were saying goodbye on the street after school.

'Can I?' Oleg's eyes lit up.

'Come to the service entrance at 7.30 sharp. Come in and wait there.'

Oleg arrived early and walked completely around the circus, found the sign saying 'Service entrance', stepped in carefully and waited inside the door.

At 7.30 Akhmet, dressed in a black felt Caucasian cloak embroidered with beads, came up to the caretaker and putting his hand on Nemets's shoulder said importantly: 'This one's with me!'

They went up to the upper floor, ran down a long corridor then climbed a spiral staircase, struggling past boxes filled with props. Following after Akhmet, Oleg clambered up the iron stairs to a narrow catwalk and then stopped dead: in the half-dark in front of him rose the dome – the circus heaven festooned with ropes. Meanwhile, Akhmet was confidently shaking the lighting technician's hand, indicating Oleg with a backwards glance.

'Here's a friend of mine. Let him sit here, will you?'

The technician nodded. He was busy with his spotlight and didn't even glance at Oleg: he was evidently used to freeloaders being shown into his workplace. Akhmet clapped Nemets on the shoulder and disappeared.

There was twenty minutes left before the performance. It was empty in the hall, cool and semi-dark. Circus hands in green uniforms, calling back and forth, were unrolling a carpet in the ring. When their shouts had died down you could hear the growling of the tigers coming from downstairs. These were the very tigers that vividly adorned the posters not far from Vladan.

Sitting in a corner of the catwalk atop an old spotlight turned around backwards, Oleg gazed down into the ring. The hall gradually filled up with people. The technician started flicking his switches. A fat man with oil-slick hair, wearing a black tailcoat that didn't meet over his stomach, stepped forward and loudly and beautifully pronounced the familiar and mysterious word: 'Vlaaa-daaan!'

The orchestra struck up a tango. The technician beside Oleg started bustling about. The lights in the hall were extinguished. Then the spotlight beam lit up a magic carpet under the tent top, just like on the poster. A man in a black cape was sitting on the carpet. The magic carpet flew down headlong. Now the spotlight picked out a spot in the centre of the ring.

There a platform was slowly rotating. The man in the cape leaped from the carpet on to the platform. His black cape flew off and then away into the darkness along with the carpet. The performer stood there in a white shirt with a bowtie, narrow trousers and – he was barefoot. He stood motionless. He waited for the applause to die down. Then he walked all around the edge of the circular platform, bowed, and sat down in an armchair as if tired from his lengthy stroll.

The ringmaster again stepped out into the arena and announced: 'The artist who draws with his feet – Vladan!'

A bright light flashed on in the hall. The woman in the snow-white ball gown danced out into the arena to the tango. She bowed as well, and set up an easel in front of Vladan, fixing a sheet of paper on to it. Vladan raised his bare feet, and only now did it become apparent that his shirtsleeves hung down at his sides and that the sleeves were empty. The artist was drawing with his feet because he had no hands.

The orchestra fell silent. Vladan's right foot flashed over the paper; in the quiet of the hall you could hear the scraping noise of the charcoal that Vladan was drawing with. He did it very quickly. After several seconds the music struck up again. The woman removed the freshly created landscape off the easel and showed it off around the arena. Oleg was sitting higher than everyone, but even he could make out palms, the sea and houses on the shore.

And that was just the beginning! Vladan would be presented with a new sheet of paper, and he would instantly make a new sketch. By the time his assistant had circled around the platform, a new drawing would be ready. At the end of each trip the assistant handed over each picture to the audience, and the sheet of paper began its journey from hand to hand along the rows or up into the very top seats.

Oleg's head was spinning – from the height from which he had to look down on the ring and the dazzling, multicoloured lights that the technician was controlling, or maybe from the smoke and the crackling noise from the high-voltage arcs in the spotlights.

Suddenly the music broke off, and the lights in the tent were extinguished. In the spotlight beam the magic carpet flew down into the ring. It picked up Vladan and his assistant and carried them away into the darkness. The orchestra struck up a march, drowning out the noise of the applause. The spectators were applauding furiously, demanding an encore. Vladan didn't come back.

That whole evening seemed incredible to Oleg – he was at the circus for the first time in his life, after all. But neither his friend Akhmet Akhmetzhanov, casting off his felt cloak and clambering up the slender twenty-metre pole, there to do a handstand, nor the acrobat brothers Chertanov, nor the bareback riders, not even the tigers tenderly licking the face of their girl trainer – no one impressed Oleg as much as the artist without hands, Vladan.

The next afternoon, at home after school, while his mother was at work, Oleg decided to replicate Vladan's act. He tucked his hands into his pockets, sat down in a chair and tried to pick up a pencil off the floor with his toes. Nothing came of it. Then he put the pencil in between his toes with his hand and started drawing on a piece of paper he had stuck to the wall. What resulted was a joke: his foot stubbornly disobeyed him and didn't want to create a masterpiece. Lyuska was sitting next to him, dying of laughter. His mother found out about his experiment and said that Oleg was going crazy. Even his father had never done anything like that, and he was an artist, after all. Oleg answered that if she had gone to the circus she would be giving it a try as well.

'As if I had time for the circus or anything else!' his mother exclaimed.

Akhmet took Oleg along to the circus a lot. His mother didn't object, thinking it was better for him to be sitting backstage than wandering the streets with God-knows-who. At home Oleg would repeat non-stop the satirical ditties sung by the clowns: 'Here and there – Hitler beware! Bet your boots – Hitler's *kaput!*' and other such brilliant verses. Oleg could announce the acts just like the ringmaster, without getting anything mixed up. His biggest lack was an imposing paunch that his tailcoat wouldn't go around, never mind the tailcoat itself.

Oleg felt he belonged in the circus. Vladan still remained a mysterious creature who would fly in on a magic carpet from an unknown world.

Once Akhmetzhanov senior injured an arm, and their act was cancelled for the day. Akhmet was very happy that he didn't have to perform that day and dragged Oleg off to the empty dressing-room where they crossed swords over a chessboard. Akhmet played so well that Oleg never managed to notice that his king was about to be put in check. Nemets didn't get upset, but he soon got bored at losing hopelessly time after time, the more so as a performance was going on the whole time in the ring.

'Akhmet, let's go and watch instead . . .'

'But you've seen it a dozen times!'

'Well, it's crazy to be at the circus and not be watching it!'

They were rushing down the corridor to the stairs when someone called to them.

'Akhmet!' A voice, soft and hoarse, sounded from behind them. 'Come over here!'

The children stopped.

'Vladan is calling us,' Akhmet said and went up to an open door.

In the middle of the room stood a young man of no great height in a white undershirt and wrinkled pyjama bottoms. He smiled quizzically.

'Vladan, this is my friend, Oleg Nemets.'

Akhmet nudged Oleg forward. Nemets stretched out his hand to greet him like an adult but was immediately embarrassed, since Vladan had short stumps sticking out from his shoulders instead of arms. He didn't even have any elbows. Oleg got confused, but Vladan burst out laughing and thus pardoned him right away.

'Let's get acquainted,' he introduced himself, leaning forward and bringing both stumps together at chest level, squeezing Oleg's palm with them. 'I'm Slava.'

'But where's Vladan?' Oleg asked in confusion.

'This *is* Vladan,' Akhmet chuckled. 'He's Vladan in the ring, Slava at home. What did you call us for, Slava?'

'Have you seen Maya by any chance? Where has she vanished to? I can't understand it . . . Kids, would you put my stuff away in the cupboard for me? It's getting under my feet.'

The magician who drew with his feet was standing in the middle of the room in a sleeveless undershirt, shaggy-headed and dismayed, gesticulating with the stumps of his arms, and all around him on the floor his odds and ends had been flung. Akhmet dexterously picked up the underwear and clothes and put them away in the cupboard. Oleg helped him as best he could.

'Do you want to play some chess?' Akhmet asked Vladan, when they had his room a bit tidier.

'Sure! Only with our guest first. All right?'

Oleg nodded not very confidently.

'Set the men up.'

A chessboard lay on the floor. Oleg made his move, Vladan, sitting on the couch, stretched out a foot right away and, grabbing a figure with his toes, placed it precisely on the desired square. He beat Nemets quickly and said: 'Come more often – then you'll win some.'

From that evening on, you could say Oleg became friends, sort of, with Vladislav Danilov – or Vladan, as they abbreviated it on the billboards. And he was very proud of his friendship. Oleg would run off to see Vladan almost every day, even more often than to see Akhmet. He would go on errands for him to the market for cheap tobacco and learned how to use newspaper to roll cigarettes that he would put in Vladan's mouth and then light up. He learned how to stub out the cigarette ends in a dish marked 'State Circus' that served as an ashtray. He even did his homework sitting with Vladan, while the latter fed him with whatever he had.

One afternoon Oleg ran cheerfully into Vladan's cubicle. 'Shall we play some chess?'

Vladan kept silent.

'Are you all right?'

'It's hard without any hands, brother,' he answered sadly. 'Help-lessness is humiliating. I don't want to go on living . . .'

He was gloomier than a rain cloud.

'I'd like a glass of vodka . . . Get some for me, brother, hey . . .'

Nodding his head, Oleg rushed home, remembering that his mother had stashed a bottle under the bed that she had got from God-knew-where. Luckily, nobody was home. Oleg wrapped it in a newspaper and brought it back to Vladan. He was sitting half distract-edly on his couch, still in the same pose.

'Where did you get it?'

'From my mother . . .'

'Thanks, my friend! Pour me some.'

Oleg poured him out half a glass.

'More.'

The glass was filled to the brim.

'Now put a stopper in it, wrap up the bottle in the newspaper and don't forget to take it home with you. Otherwise I'll drink the whole lot.'

Squeezing the glass in the stumps of his arms, Vladan knocked it back without spilling a drop, not grimacing or eating anything along with it, just as if it were only water. He sat and waited for the medicine to take effect. Oleg touched his stumps.

'Did this happen at the front?'

Vladan grabbed Oleg by the shoulders with his stumps and squeezed. 'I was a driver, you know. And I left my hands behind in my half-track.'

'How did you do that?' Oleg didn't understand.

'This is how. We were surrounded and trying to break out. I could feel that the tracks were sinking. We were in a bog; had to go around. We started circling around it when we ran into a minefield. I only remember the guys pulling me out, and I was yelling: 'My hands! Get my hands!' That was all . . .'

'I see,' Oleg drawled despondently.

'If you see, brother, then don't refuse me this favour: go and get Maya! You see what's going to happen? They're taking us to the front . . .'

'Taking you – to the front?'

'Our act has been included in a team that's going to be performing at the front.'

Of course, Oleg knew where Maya was staying: Vladan had sent him to her lots of times. It was rather far from the circus, beyond the railway station. If the tram wasn't running, and it very rarely did run, then it was about forty minutes on foot. So Nemets set off for Maya's place.

The more attached Oleg became to Vladan, the less understandable to him was Vladan's relationship with Maya. Vladan had met her in Tashkent, at the military hospital, where he was recovering after being wounded. The snub-nosed, freckled Maya had started coming to his ward now and again.

She was a refugee, evacuated, her entire family had been killed. She was eleven years older than Vladan. He had been conscripted into tank school out of the Surikov Academy of Art, where he had been forecast as destined for glory, the new Repin. And while Vladan was recuperating for half a year in the military hospital, he had found himself something to do: lacking hands, he would draw with his feet. Then he was picked up by a passing circus troupe, since they didn't have enough performers. Vladan persuaded Maya to come along with him.

She started out helping him at rehearsals, putting on his make-up, and then little by little started coming on stage with him. Vladan and Maya had got married at a registry office and lived in a dressing-room: they slept on the couch and ate at the dressing-table. They had passed through many a city together, but suddenly everything had broken down.

The first thing was when Maya started sticking up announcements that she herself had written out: 'The circus will rent a room for a female performer.' And she found a room. To Vladan's questions she would answer that she was leaving him to live in a house because she was tired of wandering. A house, even if it belonged to someone else, was none the less a house. She wasn't living with him any more but came to work. Here, after each performance, Oleg could hear them having their rows. Vladan would come out sullen, run into chairs and curse.

'What do you want? You want to leave me altogether? You'll be done for.'

'I'm fed up with this place . . .'

'And our act? What about our act?'

'I don't give a damn!'

Slamming the door, she left and ran into the ringmaster in the corridor. He was wearing his dress trousers, but instead of his tailcoat he was in green-striped pyjamas. The ringmaster took Maya into his arms and tried to calm her down.

'The Akhmetzhanovs are sick. You two are causing a scene. You're going to screw up the show. You could get court-martialled for this kind of thing at the front!'

Without answering, Maya tore herself free and ran off. Their act was dropped from the programme.

Oleg ran to Maya's place with great reluctance.

The door that he knocked at didn't open for a long time. Oleg was already about to go when Maya finally came out in her bathrobe, combing her long curly hair.

'Well, what do you want?' she asked wearily. 'Again? Tell Vladan that I'm not coming any more. Get it?'

'No, I don't get it!' Oleg shook his head.

'You don't get it? Then buzz off, anyway!'

A large man in underpants appeared behind Maya. Oleg knew who he was. This heavyweight was advertised as the strongman in the circus – a champion amongst strongmen. He would lift enormous barbells of unbelievable weight, and then the lights would go down, and a circus hand would gather up an armful of the weights and run out of the arena with them.

'Listen, sonny boy,' sneered the heavyweight. 'Maya is busy right now.'

'He asked me to tell you,' continued Oleg, 'that he's going off to the front . . .'

'To the front?' Maya showed surprise, then shrugged. 'Well, then, let him go! What's that got to do with me?'

Oleg ran back, tortured by doubts. What would he do: repeat Maya's words to Vladan or not? It would be hard on Vladan to hear what she had said. But if Oleg was to lie, what then?

'Well?' Vladan asked, when Oleg had scarcely come in the door.

'Maya isn't there,' Oleg said.

'Where is she then?'

'She's gone away somewhere . . . for good . . .'

Vladan compressed his lips. Oleg rolled him a cigarette, put it in his mouth and lit it.

'So that's how it is . . .' muttered Vladan.

He lay down on the couch and turned his face to the wall.

The next day the circus troupe was leaving: part of it to the front, the rest off to join another circus. Saying goodbye, Akhmet handed Oleg a new poster as a present. Instead of *Three – Akhmetzhanovs – Three*, it was now *Five – Akhmetzhanovs – Five*. Oleg inherited Vladan's drawings from him. Not the big ones that he did in the arena for the spectators but little ones that he did for himself. These drawings hung for a long time on the walls at the Nemetses'. When they were leaving for America, customs officials wouldn't let them take the drawings with them, so Oleg had ripped them up, out of sheer pique.

Deafened slightly by the thunderous music, Nemets sat in the circus, his head sunk into his shoulders and his palms pressed to his ears. Time had turned around again and come rushing back. Ninel was looking at Oleg in alarm, without understanding what had happened. In the arena a young woman was taking the landscapes made by the artist, half lying in an armchair and drawing with his feet, off the easel. The empty sleeves of his white shirt flapped in the draughts of air. The performer who had flown down on the magic carpet in his black cape had gone white-haired, though.

Really excited now, Oleg could barely see what was going on in the arena, and as soon as the act was finished he stood up.

'I . . . well, I've got to go backstage,' he said incoherently to Ninel. 'Got to talk to that man . . .'

'And is everything all right with your heart?'

'It's all right . . . Don't worry . . .'

And Nemets walked down the aisle, now and then bumping against someone's legs and mechanically excusing himself the while.

An elderly black cleaner, when she discovered what he was after, pointed out the door to him.

In front of a mirror, with his back to Oleg, sat an old man with a mane of white hair, and a woman in a white apron was holding a paper cup to his lips so that he could drink from it. Oleg waited while the old man drank his fill.

'Slava,' Oleg said quietly.

'Here I am,' the man answered cheerfully and turned around in his swivel chair.

'Once you answer to that name, it means it has to be you.'

'Of course it's me. But, excuse me, who are you?'

'It's a bit difficult for me to explain . . . I'm the little jerk that you played chess with and . . . sent after Maya . . . My name is Oleg Nemets.'

For some time they silently and studiously looked at each other.

'The war?' Vladan asked like someone asking for a secret password.

'The war,' confirmed Oleg and sighed.

'Since this is your friend, I'll be back in a few minutes,' the woman said in English and walked out.

'What did she say?' asked Vladan.

'She's going out for a few minutes,' Oleg translated.

'I know you're not supposed to smoke here,' Vladan winked at him. 'But as long as the lady that they've attached to me is out, get me a cigarette from that bag over there. We're mates, aren't we? How can we not smoke on such an occasion?'

Striking his lighter, Oleg lit a cigarette for Vladan and then himself lit up.

'You see, I'm at the same old gig,' Vladan said and started coughing.

'Who helps you then?'

'Whoever is handy . . . They never stick around.' Vladan suddenly burst into song. '*I've been changing my women, diddy-bump, diddy-bump, like hands through gloves . . .*'

'It's great to see you healthy and in good form, in spite of everything!'

'Healthy?!' Vladan grinned sadly. 'Aren't you surprised that I'm alive at all? After all, I'm over seventy. And you? What are you doing?'

Oleg told him in brief. He was at a loss and stupid because of it.

'You have a family, while I live as a bachelor, the way I always have, as long as you don't count the occasional episode. I don't live, I just exist . . .'

'How is Maya? Or maybe you don't to bring it all back to mind?'

'Maya, just imagine, came to our performance in New York. She's living in Brighton Beach with her husband.'

'Was he a circus performer as well?'

'Now he's a doorman at a hotel. Not a boy, after all . . . They wouldn't ever let me go abroad before – after all, Soviet people couldn't be cripples. Now it's only lazy people who don't get over here. I know that everybody moonlights, but not circus people, believe you me: on the high wire under the big tent you won't find anybody doing work on the side . . . Listen, Oleg, you've got a handle on this English stuff, after all. Take a look at what they're writing about me, here?'

With a nod of his head, Vladan indicated a sidetable. Nemets picked up the latest issue of the *San Francisco Examiner*. In the photo, Vladan was in his working pose in the ring. The headline said: 'Russian Artist Who Draws With His Foot Better Than Other Artists With Their Hands.'

'I don't read newspapers, you know.' Oleg said. 'It looks like this isn't the first time they've written about you here. Here, listen: in connection with the appearance of the talented Russian artist without any hands, the newspaper decided to have a competition for their women readers: which organ is the most important for a man to have?'

Only now did it strike Oleg what Miron's guests were arguing about.

'Which one, then?' asked Vladan, squinting at the newspaper.

'The female readership willingly responded,' Oleg translated. 'One young woman stated that the question was improperly formulated: she likes all her boyfriend's organs. One feminist proclaimed that men don't have any important organs at all, they're all second-rate, while only women have all the important organs. She was the one who won first prize in the contest: a free subscription to the *San Francisco Examiner*.'

'My God!' exclaimed Vladan.

'Here's some more,' Oleg continued to read. 'They're going to put you on television for all America to see. Get yourself ready! The famous Barbara Walters has come especially to San Francisco for an interview with you for *20/20*.'

'What do I need all this for?'

'It's too late, brother: you're a celebrity. Here are some letters from female readers. Listen up, you're being proposed to. Some Stephanie Boxer is ready to console you in your loneliness. She writes that Vladan's lack of hands isn't an obstacle and that she's ready to marry you. If you marry her, you can stay in America.'

Vladan was smiling. But there were tears in his eyes.

'What, is this for real? Nobody ever proposed any such thing to me in my life. In my youth I wanted to make love to women with my hands, too – you understand? – and suffered a lot because I couldn't . . . Maupassant said that as long as he had a single finger he was still a man, but I have neither fingers nor the things they grow from. Who needs me, a miserable cripple, a victim of that dumb, idiotic war, a stump of a man?'

I never made it because of the war, too, Oleg wanted to say. But it was inappropriate, so he didn't say it.

'Vladan, let me take you home with us,' he said instead. 'You can take a break . . . Relax . . . Walk along a beach . . . And then I'll bring you back. All right?'

'No, Oleg, no! None of that is for me. I have only two points of existence: the ring and my dressing-room and couch. And I'll die either here or there. Now goodbye, my good friend. I have to take my sedative and go to bed.'

'Then here is my telephone number.' Oleg scribbled his number on a scrap of paper. 'After you've had your rest, give me a ring, and I'll come pick you up and . . .'

Vladan nodded. Oleg hugged him, understanding that no phone call would ensue. The empty sleeves of Vladan's snow-white shirt swayed and hung still.

Oleg went out. The performance was long over, and the area around the circus had emptied out. The sun – orange, heavy and indifferent – was sinking into the Pacific Ocean. There was no difference between it and the sun that Oleg had seen in the village on the eve of the war.

Ninel was standing, lonely, at the entrance, waiting for her husband.

# APARTMENT NO. 1

Oleg Nemets had seen a lot of the world. But he had never had the opportunity of getting back to the town where he had been born. There was an objective impediment to it now, since Oleg had moved to another continent long before and become an American citizen. He kept hoping to go there on tour, but his orchestra had never set foot in the place.

And now on a free day before their departure after their last concert in Moscow, stuffy and full of petrol fumes, Oleg realized distinctly that if he didn't immediately set out for the place he would never see his native town again. He came to an agreement with his wife, who was nattering blissfully from morning till night with her old girlfriends, to meet her at ten o'clock that evening at the entrance to the Central Telegraph Office.

Of course, there were no tickets for the early flight from Bykovo Airport. But for the close-shaved, impressive-looking gentleman, dressed in an entirely un-Russian manner, with an American passport and – most important – for twice the price in hard currency, a ticket had been found, by chance. Soon Oleg was passing through the magnetic traps on his way to board the plane. If everything turned out all right, it would be less than an hour's flight, and he would have several hours there.

In the trembling aircraft Nemets dozed in his seat, tight for his thickening body, and calculated how long it had been since he had seen his native town. It came out to be about half a century. In the general history of mankind his voyage had no substantive significance, but history doesn't happen on its own. It either flows past us or drags us into the whirlpool. We struggle out of it, dry off in the sunshine, and it seems that history once again flows independently past. It can flow easily enough without us, but we can't live outside of it. Such philosophical themes come only into the heads of people in airborne idleness. Well, anyway, it hadn't been an easy day: it had been one full of presentiment.

The plane landed when the day had heated up to its scorching maximum. Without coming out of the squat provincial airport building, Nemets slung his bag and raincoat over his shoulder and first of all squeezed himself into line as close to the cashier as possible. He handed a dollar to the outraged old man behind him, and the latter was moved to temper justice with mercy. For three bundles of Russian banknotes Oleg purchased a return ticket on the evening flight to Moscow. He had been lucky so far. In order to rid himself of worldly cares once and for all, he bought two portions of terrible meat dumplings – they looked like boiled mice – at a café across from the airport building. He couldn't bring himself to eat them, though, so he handed them to a poor woman who expeditiously poured them into her plastic bag.

Nemets hailed a taxi and within half an hour found himself in the centre of town, strolling in pensive obedience to his internal compass.

Oleg didn't recognize anything but found his way to the old cast-iron bridge without asking anyone. He slowed his steps at the bridge. The thick metal railing, its rust painted over, was bumpy with blisters. Right here, beyond the turn, should be a kiosk, and a little further on a woman wearing a white apron, her little stand in front of her, full of multicoloured, syrup-filled sweets for three kopeks apiece. The Nemetses, father and son, would come past for a stroll. The son would bump along the cobblestones on his two-wheeler. At the kiosk, he would lean his bike against the railing. His father would get a mug of beer, and with the change his son would buy a syrup-filled sweet from the woman. Oleg would suck the sweets just right, so that they wouldn't break open too soon. As soon as the jam oozed out, the sweet was done for.

Oleg could taste the somewhat sour jam in his mouth, but after turning the corner he saw neither the beer kiosk nor the woman hawking sweets: they had stood here before the war. Instead of cobblestones, asphalt spread everywhere, and the asphalt had long ago managed to acquire snaky patterns of cracks. Nemets quickened his pace. He was already getting close.

They had been living in a narrow, crooked side street next to the Church of Andrew The First-Called. The church had been half ruined back then, its brickwork showing from underneath the plaster, and iron girders were sticking out of the belfry on the side closest to the dome. The bells had been removed by order of Peoples' Commissar for Heavy Industry Ordzhonikidze. The onion domes had long since been exposed, and the wind had borne away their iron shingles. The crosses still stood back then, as if embarrassed, leaning their shoulders forward, as if better to see the whole crooked lane.

Every day Oleg and his friends had hung around the barred windows of the church. Inside it, in compartments separated from one another by low plywood partitions, sculptors and artisans were working, moulding statues out of plaster. Through the squares of the grilles in the windows they could see unfinished monuments to their leaders – without arms, torsos or even busts. Lenin held his own head in his outstretched hand, as if he had removed it himself to take a break from the intensity of his thought about mankind's fate.

But the boys weren't crowding up to the windows for Lenin's sake. The most exciting spectacle was when they succeeding in getting a peek at the process of creating statues of weavers and collective-farm girls, Labour's shock-troops. On a raised platform alongside the monument, for fifty kopeks an hour, stood a well-endowed model who, in contrast to the statue, was wearing no clothes. The spectators at the window, shoving each other in their struggle for the best spot, commented aloud on the show.

The model as a rule paid no attention to the ragamuffins and would chatter away or sometimes would go behind a curtain and would there engage – now with one sculptor, now with another – in still another kind of art, about which Oleg had only an altogether vague idea. Sometimes the sculptors would let the two eldest children inside. They would knead the clay or bring water from the hydrant in the street, trying to get as close to the model as possible and, if they were lucky, touch her with an elbow. She would laugh out loud and say sternly: 'Come on, close your mouths – you'll get flies in them. Haven't you ever studied anatomy at school?'

The plaster on the house that Oleg and Lyuska grew up in had run with rusty stripes from the rain, but the walls were sturdy. In the previous century there had been a lot of fires in this town – there were burnt-out sites all around – but this house had remained in one piece. It had seen Napoleon.

A porch of rotten boards with a fretwork overhang led to their apartment. Lyuska with the tiny Oleg and their cat would sit on the worn-out steps and purr in trio in the sunshine. A slot had been cut into the dilapidated door. Above the slot his father had beautifully written 'Apt. No. 1' in oil paint. The postman would stick their newspapers through the slot, and they would drop into the little corridor. The bell above the slot would tinkle merrily when you twisted the little handle.

The room's glory was an antique tile oven, which their mother had to stoke from out in the corridor. At the window, blocking off the sill with its back, stood a couch. His father and mother slept on it. Two beds were squeezed along the other wall, Lyuska's and Oleg's. A flimsy bookshelf adjoined them, and on it was a wooden box that produced scratchy-sounding music. When people came to visit, their father would boast about what distant radio stations they could pick up on their new receiver – sometimes even Leningrad.

Oleg liked having guests more than anything in the world. How could such huge crowds of people manage to squeeze into the Nemetses' flat? His father was merriest in the noisiest company. He would make fun of everyone, including himself, would sing arias from operas, dance waltzes with the children in his arms. Whenever he stopped smiling, he would become serious and say, as if in justification: 'Very funny!'

Sometimes Oleg wouldn't understand his jokes; it seemed to him that his father was offending his mother. But she would clap him resoundingly on the back and laugh. His father worked as a photographic retoucher. The tools of his trade were a thin brush, a piece of frosted glass stained with Indian ink and a magnifying glass. He would bring home piles of photographs from the publishers. Oleg would cut out attractive faces from the discarded photos.

Once upon a time someone rang the doorbell. Two men in NKVD uniforms came in. His father turned white as a sheet, and, pressing her hands to her throat, his mother gulped so much air it seemed as though she was stocking up on it.

'Citizen Nemets? Let's go into your room,' one of the men said to his father. 'And you, Citizeness Nemets, take your children for a walk.'

'What do you mean?' their mother asked.

'Surely I said it in Russian? Get out.'

Sobbing hopelessly, their mother dressed the children and took them out into the yard. It was obvious that they were taking their father in. It was 1937. But then an hour and a half later the NKVD men left. One of them even saluted their mother on his way out. She ran into the flat, ready for the worst. Their father was sitting quietly at his workplace, leaning forward, elbows on the table, staring vacantly at the wall. He wouldn't answer their mother's questions, as if struck dumb. But he finally told their mother about what had happened in their home. She kept silent about it for twenty years and then told Oleg, as if recalling it by accident.

As it turned out, the NKVD men had sat his father at his desk and stood on either side of him, as if getting ready to twist his arms. One of them opened a briefcase and pulled out a large envelope sealed with wax, opening it up. On the desk in front of Oleg's father lay a photograph, a close-up of a moustachioed face pocked with smallpox scars.

It hadn't been hard to recognize the face, since it stared out of the pages of every newspaper – without the scars, of course.

'We have information that you're the best retoucher in the business,' said the other uninvited guest. 'Can you remove the unsightly bits?'

'Certainly I can,' his father barely managed to say.

'Do it!'

'But that's a lot of work.'

'We're not in a hurry . . .'

They stood over him, keeping an eye on his every movement, while he worked slowly, since his hands were shaking. When the smallpox traces had disappeared and the skin on the cheeks had become as smooth-looking as a baby's, one of the visitors dexterously pulled the photograph from under Oleg's father's elbow and tucked it into his briefcase. They placed a document in front of his father, on which he was told to write that he had been entrusted with a state secret, the disclosure of which would be punished to the fullest extent of Soviet law. Later on, Oleg's mother recalled that she and her husband had never seen anywhere a photograph taken of that face at such close range. His father supposed that the forbidden photograph had been pulled out in connection with some new statuary project but that the sculptors were not being allowed to see the real face.

'You didn't, God forbid, leave any pockmarks on him by accident?' his wife had asked in alarm later. 'They'll come to get you, for sure!'

But nothing came of it.

His father loved nothing better than clicking a shutter. He would print the photographs at night, putting the bath trays on the table alongside the children's beds. You would raise an eyelid, and there would be this strange reddish light. One photograph hung on their wall: his mother, Lyuska and their laughing father sitting on their couch. Oleg stood alongside, holding a bow and violin in his hands. Their father had sat them down then on the couch, set up his camera on its tripod, stretched his cord over to the couch and sat himself down as well.

'Hey, say "cheese", like you're supposed to!' his father yelled, roared with laughter and pulled on the cord.

The magnesium flared, the shutter clicked. Everyone was smiling the way they should except for Oleg, who was looking nervously at the cord. And that's how it came out.

The war had started in tiny ways for Oleg. They were ordered to hand over their radio to the post office and got a receipt for it. After the first air-raids his father had said: 'You'll have to be evacuated.'

Oleg liked that. Somebody blurted out to him that in the Urals, where they were sending the trains full of children, there were a lot of semi-precious stones, and Oleg was going there to pick up the beautiful gems. His mother wept. His father had stayed behind on the platform. Painters were being formed into a group to paint green and yellow spots on the roofs to camouflage them. Retouchers were counted as painters.

Their mother with her two children had been taken to a small town, quiet and poor with green front-garden fences. The caulking hung down in long strands from the log walls of their little room. Their mother would run home from work when Oleg's and the adolescent Lyuska's eyes would be stuck together from darkness and hunger. Turning her face away from the smoke, their mother would get their stove going, then do her cooking, and while they demolished the food she would warm their blankets at the stove, dreamily repeating: 'You just wait, our father will be home soon . . .'

The postman brought letters from their father, sometimes two or three at once. Oleg cut the stamps off the envelopes. Envelopes without stamps started coming later; then letters just folded into a triangle. Soon the triangles stopped coming as well. Falling asleep, Oleg could see his mother sitting on her stool, rooted to the spot, staring at the dying embers.

The war ended. That summer, the three of them had returned to their native town. Instead of a porch with its fretwork overhang, there was just a door. Their mother suddenly turned pale, squeezing Oleg's hand, and stood for a long time without moving. Above the slot that had served as their mailbox, although the paint had peeled a little bit, you could make out 'Apt. No. 1' painted in their father's hand.

Their mother collected herself, set down their suitcase and, reaching for the handle, pulled on it. The door didn't open; she tried twisting the doorbell – it barely made a scraping noise.

Lyuska pointed out something high on the wall to Oleg. The windows of their flat were gone, and the wall itself was completely new and crookedly built of broken pieces of brick and leaning out of true. Because of it the building looked like a squatter's hovel and had altogether ceased resembling the mansions seen by the Emperor Napoleon.

Leaving the children to look after the suitcase, their mother went around the corner and knocked at a neighbour's flat. A woman came out of it, dressed in an angora scarf. She unwillingly explained that the old tenants had scattered in all directions at the beginning of the war. New ones had moved in. A bomb had fallen here in the very first year of the war and had destroyed part of the building. There was nowhere to move the tenants to, and the cracks had crept further up the walls. They had patched up the wall so that the building wouldn't fall down, and in fact there was now no longer any Apartment No. 1. That was to say, the door was still there, but it didn't go anywhere. The porch had long since been chopped up for firewood.

The woman stepped back inside and locked the door thoroughly behind her. Their mother stood in confusion, shifting her weight from one foot to the other. Oleg and Lyuska looked at her, but what could she say?

Their Aunt Polina, their mother's second cousin, gave them refuge for a while. She hadn't gone anywhere and had looked after her flat the entire war long. She was living by herself at the edge of town, but, just the same, the Nemetses couldn't think of anything but a kennel of their own.

Their mother couldn't get them registered in the town, since they didn't have their own apartment, and they wouldn't put them in the queue for an apartment without registration and a reference from work. Nobody was hired for work without a registration. But they did give them back the radio that they had confiscated at the beginning of the war in exchange for the receipt that they had entirely accidentally managed to hold on to. They hadn't wanted to give it back, since the receipt was in their father's name, and he had disappeared without trace. The rest of their lives depended on their registration.

Hopelessly, their mother would trudge to the housing administration, and finally the passport-office lady, Zoya Ivanovna, took pity on them and hinted that if they greased the local inspector's palm he would turn a blind eye to the fact that Apartment No. 1 didn't really exist and would register them there.

'But how would I give him the money?' his mother asked. 'What if he doesn't take it?'

'Well, the same way everyone does,' the passport lady seemed surprised. 'Put it in a children's book and say, "Here's a present for your children."'

His mother borrowed some money from Polina and gave the local inspector a present of the book *Uncle Styopa*, into which she had put all her cash. The inspector was fat and middle-aged.

'I'll read it,' he said, puffing out his cheeks.

A week later, when Oleg's mother came by for the answer, the inspector, examining her passport, said strictly that it was nearly possible to get her registered now, but that the deputy chief in charge of passport procedures was confused by her name, with its apparent meaning of 'German'.

'Well, that's the only one I've got,' his mother explained impassively for the thousandth time.

'Maybe it's got mixed up with your nationality? If that's so, what sort of Germans would be in this town after the war? But the chief likes children's books, too . . .'

There wasn't anyone to borrow money from. His mother took off her watch and laid it on the inspector's desk. He winced but quickly put it away in the desk drawer. In a week Oleg's mother's passport had a registration stamp for Apartment No. 1, the one that didn't exist.

His mother found a job as an accountant in some sort of cooperative. What else could she have got with such a terrible last name?

Oleg realized that his father was never coming back, although no death certificate was ever forthcoming. His mother grew quiet; her hands grew rough. They lived a half-starved existence, because their mother spent her first two pay cheques on a cracked violin from a second-hand shop. Oleg glued it back together himself and all of a sudden took to playing it without any urging. Whenever he put the violin aside for a while or ran into trouble at school, his mother's eyes would fill with tears. She wouldn't say a word, just turn away quickly. Sometimes she would weep for no apparent reason.

'You're always on about just one thing: the children, the children,' Polina lectured her. 'You've got to think about yourself!'

Their mother didn't answer, as if she hadn't heard.

They lived for some time in Polina's communal apartment. Then one evening the local inspector came by. Puffing, he asked permission to sit down (saying he had been on his feet the whole day), but he had to take a look at everyone's papers. Polina wasn't there, their mother had just sent the children to bed, and Oleg was pretending that he was already asleep. But the inspector didn't even open the passport that their mother had placed on the table.

'Is there anything around here to drink?' he asked suddenly.

The request made their mother a lot happier: he wasn't going do anything; he was just going to drink up and be gone. He unstoppered the quarter-bottle of vodka that was set down in front of him and poured half a glass of it into himself, nibbled a crust of bread that lay on the table, then poured the rest of it into his glass and drank it down.

'Great!' he said, turning all red and unbuttoning his overcoat.

'Well, thanks be to God,' muttered their mother. 'Our papers are all in order, you don't have to worry about them.'

'And how about your womanly side?' He squeezed her hand.

'In what sense?' She was dumbstruck.

'Well, the direct sense. I'm a strong man – you know yourself what I want.'

He stood up, swaying, and grabbed their mother's other hand. She pulled away as far as she could.

'No, don't, please – the children can see us,' she wailed.

'Then let's go out to the corridor – don't worry, I'll spread my overcoat on the floor; it's warm.'

At that moment Polina quietly entered the room.

'Oh, you've got a party going on here,' she spoke up, having taken in the whole thing at first glance. 'But now it's time for you to go, dear guests: your hostess has to get her sleep. She's got to be at work at first light tomorrow.'

'Fine, I'll come another time,' the inspector said gloomily, letting go of their mother's hands and setting off for the door with an unsteady gait.

Burying her face against Polina's shoulder, their mother burst into sobs.

A week later the inspector came by again, but this time she had her rebuff ready. He downed his dose and then tried to get his paws on her, but she had enlisted Oleg in her defence. Hugging her arms around him, she kept him in front of her. The inspector grew furious and grabbed the empty bottle from the table, smashing it on the floor.

'It'll be the worse for you now!' he declared to her. 'Your neighbours have long since let the police know that you live in one place and are registered in another.'

He slammed the door, and everything stayed quiet for a few days.

Their mother was already on her way to bed when somebody rang their doorbell. Two policemen had come, one in civilian clothes. They confiscated her passport, telling her to come and collect it. She soon got her passport back. Their registration had been cancelled. Their mother was handed a document for her signature, saying that within forty-eight hours she had to leave the city, along with her children, and that, if she stayed, they would put her in gaol for violation of passport procedures and her children would be sent to a children's colony.

'Son,' their mother resolved, 'I want to get your advice on something . . . You're the only man around.' She had never spoken to Oleg like this before.

'I don't know what to do.' She fell silent, looking for words. 'They're evicting us. I went to the village where we used to spend our summers. I was thinking maybe that Pasha would take us in. But she's been dead for two years . . . Should we rent different places here and hide out? I've been trying to find somewhere. As soon as they ask me my name, they start laughing, and as soon as they find out we're not registered here they get scared and turn me down. And wherever I go it's always your father, your father . . . Here's the embankment – we used to go skiing there. Over there is the building where I gave birth to you and he brought me flowers. There's nowhere here that doesn't spell your father . . .'

'What do you want?'

Although Oleg considered himself nearly adult, and it had been a long time since his mother had called him by his baby name, he still couldn't suggest anything.

'They're making us evacuate for the second time,' his mother said despairingly. 'Then the Germans were to blame, but now it's because our name means "German". Let's go back to where we lived during the war. Our father was still alive for us there . . . Remember how angry he would get when I called you "Olya", like a girl? I don't call you that now.'

Oleg hadn't understood everything she was saying at the time. It didn't make any difference to him where they lived. His hooligan friends were all still there, the ones that he had played war with in people's gardens, skated with in winter, hitching on to passing trucks with wire hooks, pulling up carrots from their neighbours' allotments in summer. Here he hadn't had time to make real friends with anyone.

The neighbourhood was a den of thieves. Some were fresh out of the camps, some were on their way there. Both types would call you 'Fritz' and beat you up. Lyuska, too, was dying to go, right away: her almost-bridegroom, Nefyodov, was back there.

The Nemetses went back. Lyuska soon got married and bore two daughters. Oleg graduated from the music school that had opened after the war and made it into the symphony orchestra of the provincial philharmonic society. He got married, too, and had a son. Once the first violinist, the philharmonic society's Party secretary, said to Oleg while they were having a drink together after a concert: 'If you want to get ahead, join the Party. You're not going to become a good musician without the Party.'

It was necessary to be taken into the Party obediently – why not join if they promised you the moon? And, in fact, he was soon made third violin. To fulfil their plan, the orchestra had to tour local collective farms and military units, to afford mastery of classical music to the masses. Within five years Nemets the Communist had earned his own apartment. Soon after, he had purchased furniture and installed the collected works of Russian and progressive Western classic authors on his bookshelves, to be like everyone else. Several years further on he built himself a little summer house on his Philharmonia-allotted plot. He was in line for a Moskvich car. His son Valesha was gradually approaching the same age Oleg had been just before the war.

You couldn't say that Oleg was living happily, although it wasn't bad. You could say that he was better off than a lot of others, but his energetic wife, Ninel, who had graduated from the Plekhanov State Economics Institute in Moscow and worked as a senior economist in a planning institute, said to him one day: 'Answer me this, would you please. Who is the man in our family?'

'Let's say it's me,' Oleg said carefully. 'Why?'

'And who's the German, the Nemets, in this family?'

'Well, that's just a family name . . .'

'No matter which way you look at it, it's still you. Of course, it'd be better if you were a real German or Jew, but what can you do? So you're the man, you're the German, but it's me who has to stand in these Russian queues. And I'm fed up!'

'There's something here I don't get,' he mumbled, even though he had already worked it out. 'What are you driving at? You want a divorce? Do you want to get yourself a more euphonious name?'

'Not at all. I'm thinking of America or at any rate Germany,' his wife said. 'Everyone's getting out.'

'Really?' asked Oleg, who was, in practical life, a long way from anything but sawing on the fiddle. 'But why?'

'Because they're letting people go,' she explained comprehensively.

It was a mighty strong argument.

'Of course, I've already been digging around,' Ninel continued her advance. 'It's mostly Jews that they're letting out, but Germans and Armenians are going, too. If we get industrious enough, I think we could get an invitation as well with a surname like ours. We'll put down that you're not only a German but a Jew as well. And I'll go along with whatever you like. Just think about it: we get away, and you'll never see another registry permit as long as you live!'

That was enough to finish off his indecisiveness.

Oleg left the Party with as much ease as he had joined it. He got sacked at once from the Philharmonic Society, at his own desire supposedly. It was a good time to leave the country; it was the period of so-called détente, and the Nemetses, after waiting for several months, received amongst the general stream of people an invitation from a hitherto-unknown aunt in Israel. Nobody knew if she was an aunt or an uncle, but God grant her or him long years of life. Lyuska stayed behind with her Nefyodov and their daughters. But his mother, after some hesitation, came along with them.

In the face of Oleg's excessive modesty, it only then became obvious that he wasn't just talented but very much so – since orchestras in his new homeland didn't hang on to mediocre musicians. Since that time he had travelled the world in the three different orchestras that he had worked in, but no one in any of the countries he had been in except for the first one had ever laughed at Oleg Nemets for having a name like his. And as far as his son Valesha was concerned – he had graduated from university in America and was working as a computer engineer – the problem didn't exist at all: the Russian word *nemets* doesn't mean a thing in English, and even if it did – so what? The word closest to it, *nemesis*, means retribution or punishment. You could divine a certain symbolism in all this if you wanted to, but it doesn't really work that way in practice.

What did work was that Oleg Nemets was unaccountably drawn back to the place where he had been born, to Apartment No. 1. He had spent his life in apartments with various numbers, but he had only the one first one. However stupid this sounds, maybe it was because he had been registered there.

Oleg didn't need any registry permits any more. And he travelled around the world without needing a visa. He only needed a visa to enter the country where he had once been registered – had to pay money to dour officials to hand him a piece of paper allowing him to visit his homeland.

Marching around in the heat in his suit and tie, Oleg was soon soaked. He pulled off his jacket, rolling it up in his raincoat and unbuttoned his collar: he didn't have enough air; it was difficult to breathe. But when there was a single block between him and his home Oleg couldn't hold back any longer and lengthened his stride, bursting into a trot. He probably didn't have to rush: if they hadn't torn down the building in the intervening half-century it would stay there for another five minutes.

The building still stood. Nemets stopped and caught his breath. The lane had been turned into a dead end. A new street stretched to one side, along the embankment. Behind the church, blocking the thoroughfare, a concrete building had gone up, all glass and aluminium. Judging from the abundance of cars at its entrance and the policemen milling around it, it was an institution of some gravity.

The church was surrounded by trees. The crooked crosses had been straightened, the onion domes had been shingled with tin-plate and painted bright yellow, in substitution for the gilt. Oleg looked into a window through the grating. Sculptors and sculptures had disappeared. Inside stood toilet bowls and boxes of bathroom tiles – it was now a storage facility. Oleg could have been too late: bulldozers were massed in a bunch near by. Pretty soon there would be nothing of the street left except for the church, on which had appeared a plaque like something on a gravestone: 'Preserved by the Government. Damage Punishable by Law'. Although there was nothing left to damage.

Their apartment door, as before, hung above the ground. And you could still make out the sign 'Apt. No. 1'. The door was nailed shut with crossed planks. Nemets walked around the building, tripping over broken bricks; with curiosity he examined the new wall cutting off that part of the building and made up his mind to ring the doorbell of Apartment No. 2.

For a long time nobody opened the door, but then he heard an elderly voice: 'What do you want?'

'I'm from the construction department,' said Oleg, the first thing to come into his mind, trying to turn his quiet voice into a rough businesslike one.

'So what do you want?' repeated the voice behind the door.

'About the demolition . . . We're examining the building.'

Two locks were turned and the bolt shot back. An old woman in a dirty smock that had once had a flower pattern on it looked Oleg over suspiciously. But he was decently dressed and there was nothing criminal written on his face.

'The building's rotten and we're demolishing it,' Nemets said sternly. And, trying not to attach any significance to his words, added: 'Why is the door of the first apartment nailed shut?'

They were standing on either side of the threshold. The woman didn't answer for a long time. Sticking her hairclip in her mouth, she pulled her hair back tight. Holding on to the door with one hand, she stretched her neck out to have a look at the door of Apartment No. 1 as if noticing it for the first time. And then she said what Oleg had already known for a long time: the building had been bombed in the war, cracks were running up the walls, and they had put up a new wall just there.

'Can I come in and have a look to see if there are any cracks there, Granny?'

'Come on in, since you're the boss. Only I ain't tidied up here since last night.'

The squalor and dirt in the room he entered was monumental. 'You have been listening to marches and songs of the motherland,' the radio announcer happily declared. Oleg carefully examined the wall separating the old woman's musty abode from the non-existent Apartment No. 1. He looked through a window with rusty iron bars and grasped that her wall didn't go all the way to the new brickwork. There was a space left over, a part of the building that you couldn't enter.

For appearance's sake Oleg took out a notebook and scribbled a flourish in it, thanking the old woman. She asked if they were going to transfer her to a new place soon and how long they were going to keep on promising it to her.

'Soon,' Oleg reassured her. But he couldn't resist saying, 'Don't even worry about cleaning the place up.'

'That's what I think, too,' the woman agreed. 'Why bother cleaning if they're chucking me out? You've got my gratitude, dearie.'

'Not at all!'

Oleg searched out the local locksmith at the housing office. He was in sturdy good health but a bit bloated from cheap Russian fruit-flavoured wine, and he was half lying on an old couch in a small room with a washbasin and toilet. This beefy locksmith couldn't grasp what his visitor wanted from him for a long time. He grumbled that people were twisting his arm for all sorts of nonsense, when his big problem was leaky toilet cisterns.

'What do you need this door for, for God's sake? Tell me, and I'll let you in . . .'

Oleg pulled a plastic bag with a thick wad of money in it out of his pocket.

'That enough?'

Proletarian pride flared in the beefy locksmith's eyes, but not long enough to give his customer the opportunity to change his mind.

'Well, that's a start,' the locksmith said edifyingly, carelessly stashing the bag of dried roubles in his pocket. 'Everybody looking for something, but it's just me here.'

They took a backyard passage that Oleg had no suspicion of. The passage hadn't existed previously. They stopped at Apartment No. 1. The locksmith set his case down on the ground and looked the door over.

'This is a big deal,' he said, jacking his price up. 'Got to think this over first.'

He lit a cigarette unhurriedly. Oleg waited. Then he took out his own cigarettes and, snapping his lighter, lit up as well.

'Who you be, yourself?'

'Fiddle player.'

'Wow, hot stuff!' the locksmith roared out laughing. 'A fiddler . . . we're all fiddling. You a professional or what? Yeah, I could see your wallet bulging. Hey, there ain't no kind of antiques behind that damned door! It's stayed the way it was when they nailed it shut in the war.'

Tossing his butt away, the vanguard of the revolution kicked his case, and it sprang open. He pulled a large bundle of keys on a wire out of it.

'Maybe you should pull the boards off first?' Nemets suggested carefully.

'The boards are fine.'

The locksmith started trying out the keys. Not one of them fitted or maybe the lock had just rusted up. Looking askance at Oleg the locksmith took his time. The possibility that this was some kind of dirty trick alarmed him. If there wasn't anything there, why would he have been advanced a whole bundle, for God's sake, and not just a couple of bills as per usual?

'What's your last name, then?'

'Nemets.'

'From Germany, huh?'

'I'm telling you, my family name is Nemets.'

'That's a funny last name . . . Are you Jewish or something? What the hell do you want to root around in there for? They're going to tear it down soon. Just come on over then and take a look.'

'I'm just here on a visit.'

'Where from?'

'San Francisco. On tour here . . .'

'Moonlighting, is that it? Like they say, you used to be a traitor to the motherland, and now you're our friend and brother. Show me your damned passport . . .'

Oleg handed over his blue passport with a grin. With curiosity the locksmith turned it this way and that.

'Something here ain't the way we do it. So what the hell nationality are you?'

'American.'

'But you say your last name is Nemets. Weird!'

The interrogation was getting to be a bore.

'Well? Are you going to unlock it or . . .'

Oleg was fed up. He snatched his passport out of the locksmith's hand and pulled a screamer out of his pocket, a little case with a police siren in it, that someone had advised him to buy before his departure for Russia.

'What the hell is that thing?' the locksmith said in surprise.

'Now I'm going to zap you with this ray gun – you'll be impotent. Hand over the money, I'll find somebody else. Want me to turn this on?'

I'm the boss, here.' The man was offended. 'Why you coming on so tough?'

The locksmith bent over and pulled a hatchet out of his case. Nails groaned, planks crashed to the ground. Wedged into the doorjamb, the hatchet squealed and, breaking off splinters, caught hold of the door. It squeaked, wheezed and opened. A gust of damp and rot came out.

'Go on in, get your fancy threads dirty, it's your party . . .'

Biting his lip in agitation, Oleg stepped across the threshold. Cobwebs hung in dusty garlands from the ceiling, moving like something alive. Under the layer of brick chips and rubbish on the floor pieces of paper could be seen. Oleg picked them up, shook them and wiped them with his palm. They were two letters that had been dropped through the letterbox in the door and never picked up by anyone. One was triangular, the other was in an envelope. He jammed them into his pocket and, pulling his head down into his shoulders, stepped forward.

It was dark in the little corridor covered with brick and concrete chips. The door from the corridor into the room was off its hinges, the doorway blocked by a fallen girder. Oleg couldn't shift the girder to one side, so he just wormed his way under it, getting all dirty. Beyond that, it was utter darkness. Stretching his hands out in front of him like a blind man Oleg took one step and then another. Underfoot, things creaked and crunched. He felt for the lighter in his pocket, snapped it alight. He tore off a strip of unstuck wallpaper from the wall, lit the edge of it and when it caught fire dropped it on the floor.

The flame grew slowly. Then the whole piece of wallpaper flared into flame, illuminating the worn-down floorboards that had once been painted. Oleg raised his eyes: in front of him sat a part of their tiled stove, scored by shrapnel. He had noticed the gilded, multi-coloured delft tiles in his earliest memories; the pictures on them had caught his attention somewhat later. Blue musicians. Blue ladies a-dance with blue cavaliers. Taking their leave after the ball – blue carriages and blue horses.

Only now did Oleg glance at the floor and realize what he had been crushing underfoot. Below lay pieces of white glass with black stains. He picked up some fragments of the glass with the letter in his hand and poured them into his pocket.

The wallpaper strip was burning out. Oleg tore another strip off the wall, ripped it in half, and threw it on to the fire. Flakes of soot flew up. There was a smell of burnt paint from the floor. Now he could see that the new wall – crooked and hastily laid of brick fragments – began from the stove itself. The remaining space between the walls was narrow, around a metre and a half, and in the depths shrank to nothing, running into the wall of the old woman's apartment. In the space, bent and pressed against the wall, were two rusty beds – Lyuska's and Oleg's. A flare-up of the fire just before dying lit up the dark rectangle over the bed. Oleg couldn't succeed in tearing the photograph from the wall, although he tore his nails trying, it was so firmly stuck. His mother had usually grumbled whenever his father stuck photographs on the wall. But his father would answer:

'Wallpaper is craft, a photograph is art . . .'

Squinting, Nemets came back outside. The locksmith sat on his case, smoking.

'Give me your knife!' ordered Oleg.

The locksmith raised an eyebrow but silently stood and pulled a knife – rather, a sharpened piece of a saw, half of it wrapped in insulating tape – out of his case. Oleg tried to set another strip of wallpaper alight, but however hard he tried to get his lighter going the fuel in it was exhausted. His hands touching the walls, Oleg moved forward and, feeling the photograph on the wall, thrust the knife between the wallpaper and the plaster, cutting it off with a good bit to spare. He carried the photo out into the sunlight and, when his eyes had grown accustomed to it, could see that he had hardly damaged it at all, except for cutting off one tiny corner.

The locksmith smoked, sitting on his case in a thinker's pose.

'Do I look like him?' Oleg asked the locksmith, pointing his finger at the little boy in the white bowtie, violin in one hand and his bow in the other.

'What the hell! German, American . . . I got you right off. Lived hereabouts?'

'Before the war. And afterwards – I was registered here. Just registered but lived . . .'

'Did a spell in gaol, I bet you.' The locksmith kept to his own train of thought. 'I can see the whole thing in your face. You think your little box scared me? I felt sorry for you, that's what! All you Germans got put in the clink back then. You saw away on your fiddle now, and here we got to answer for every leaky toilet bowl.'

He looked Oleg over from head to toe, weighing him up, and then looked at the photograph again and softened somewhat.

'Wipe off the damned cobwebs!'

Nemets brushed off the shoulders of his jacket. Without interest, but just to keep from falling silent, he said: 'Do you have a family?'

'Had one somewhere.'

'What do you mean?'

'I mean, it's better not to know where so's I don't have to mess with the payments. You might be a violinist, but you're sure dim. You must get by without any kind of learning. Know what? Give me another bundle – you got that much and more in your bag, I seen it!'

It was clear that his wife was going to reproach him for this, like any other one of his impracticalities, but Oleg forked out another bundle anyway. The vanguard of the revolution perked up, lifted his hatchet and beat the door back into place with its head, nailing the planks back across each other as they had been before, then picked up his case and, without even a nod, cheerfully stamped off. After a few steps he turned around.

'Think of anything, come on back. I'm here the whole time. I'll crack her open again for you.'

'But they're tearing it down . . .'

'Oh, yeah. They've been tearing it down for years, and it still ain't gone nowhere.' The locksmith's sense of humour suddenly came to life. 'I bet you – maybe there won't be no need to tear it down,' he grinned. 'Depends on who pays what to who.'

In the neighbouring yard children were playing in the trampled flowerbed. The bench next to it, in the shade, was vacant. Oleg sat down, closed his eyes and tried to collect his thoughts. They were all going their own way. *Ssswisssshhhh!* came from behind him. The boys were breaking off branches from a lilac bush. They were breaking them off, tossing them to the ground, stamping on them and cackling. Oleg sighed, pulled out the letters that he had put in his pocket and started examining them.

The missives had warped and faded, and the triangular one was mildewed to boot. Oleg turned them over and squinted at them, trying to make out what was inscribed on them. Several words had disappeared, blue stains now in their places. A brown strip had been burnt on to the outside of the envelope. Obviously, the sun had penetrated through the letterbox. Diagonally across from it blazed the black field-post-office stamp and its number. The violet stamp with its 'Passed by Military Censor' crest looked as if it had just been done.

Oleg was in no hurry to open the letters. He got a light from a passer-by and took a long drag on his cigarette. The letters disappeared momentarily into the cloud of smoke. Oleg looked at the names on them. Both letters were addressed to his mother, but it had already been fifteen years since she had died in the hospital in San Francisco. She had been certain up to her last breath that his father was still alive. He was alive and was going to come back – despite all common sense, time, despite everything. Lyuska, giving up the grandchildren and her husband for a week, had flown to be at her funeral at Oleg's expense.

Oleg unfolded the triangular letter with a sharp movement, and it turned into a yellowed sheet from a notebook. The sender's first name and surname at the end, below the text – Viktor Rumyantsev – didn't bring anything to mind. The man who had written the letter was in the same company as Nemets senior. Their father – he wrote – had been killed right in front of his eyes, fighting for his motherland and Comrade Stalin. And the soldiers had sworn vengeance on the Germans for the death of their comrade-in-arms, who was only accidentally the possessor of such a terrible surname as Nemets. According to the stamp, it had happened no later than the end of October 1941.

The second letter had a stamp and franking from 1946, and Oleg hurriedly opened it. The sheet inside the envelope was well preserved. It was either Oleg's imagination or it really did smell of medicine.

It was the same Viktor Rumyantsev, but the handwriting was cramped and hurried. He informed them that it was already four years since he had been placed in a psychiatric hospital after getting shell-shocked. He was in entirely good health and was feeling well. But they wouldn't let him out of the hospital, because he kept on talking about the horrors that he had come through, which the doctors didn't like. But he couldn't forget, and that was all there was to it. He could not forget the fallen friend with whom he had shared bread and vodka. At the time, from the front, he hadn't written the whole truth because he was afraid to, you could get shot for it. Now they checked all letters here as well, just like at the front, but this letter was being taken away and mailed by a trustworthy nurse who wouldn't betray him.

My friend, Rumyantsev wrote, died for nothing. They launched a wave of us unarmed men at the fascists, and we were literally riddled with bullets, may he be thrice cursed, that bastard Comrade Stalin. I was saved only by the fact that I was behind my friend and myself fell down as if killed. I lay that way until dark. I pulled his wallet out of his tunic and put its contents into my own. I crossed his arms on his breast, crawled into the woods and got out back to our own side. I carefully preserved the photograph with his boy and his fiddle, his daughter and his wife. There was a postcard, too, where his father wished his son Oleg a happy birthday, that he had never managed to send.

His lips had gone dry, and Oleg licked them, blinking in dismay, then went on making out the faded words. *There was a folded piece of paper there, too,* Rumyantsev wrote, *and in it was a dried flower – probably lilac but with six petals instead of four. I thought that when the war was over I could go and see my friend's dear ones and hand it over to you, but when I got shell-shocked it disappeared along with all my clothes, and that was that. I often dream the same dream now, over and over: my friend Nemets and I are sitting in a circus, and Hitler and Stalin are fighting in the ring. They keep on striving to knock each other's teeth out or trip each other up. The audience sits in silence, without any reaction. I can never make out who is going to win – Stalin or Hitler: each time I wake up when I look behind me at the audience, because the spectators are all dead. Dead bodies, all in soldiers' uniforms. And my friend whose name means 'German' is sitting dead next to me, not joking like he always did, and always leaning, leaning against me. I have hardly enough strength to keep on holding up his corpse. There is a deathly silence in the circus. I'm the only one alive in the place.*

At the end of the letter Viktor Rumyantsev apologized for not being able to visit his friend's family and tell them everything but said that he wouldn't give up hope of getting out of the hospital, although he was losing consciousness more and more often, and would write to them as soon as he got out. There was no further letter. And it was strange that the postman had put this last one through the slot anyway: the apartment had already been bombed. Only the door remained.

Oleg tucked the letter away in his wallet and carefully turned his pocket inside out. On his palm lay shards of white glass covered with black Indian-ink stains. His father's brush had made these stains on the white glass. Whenever his father had sat down to retouch a photograph the white glass was always in front of him. The very same ink had hidden Comrade Stalin's pockmarks. Drops of blood were drying on the pieces of glass. Holding them a while longer in his palm Oleg poured them under his bench. Only now did he notice that he had cut himself when he was gathering the pieces of glass. He sucked at the scratches on two of his fingers and spat: the cut was deep.

Around the bench that he was sitting on the children were running and making a racket. The heat had died down. There was a smell of lilac. When she had come to visit Oleg in California Lyuska had straight away rushed to the lilac bush in his garden and discovered in surprise that there were as many of the lucky five- and six-petalled flowers as you could want.

'That's just the sort we have here,' Oleg laughed.

'It's just strange that there's practically no smell. But do you remember . . . ?' Lyuska hadn't finished what she was saying before tears welled in her eyes.

Oleg felt tired and shook his head to cheer himself up. He put his jacket back on and threw his raincoat over his shoulder. The photograph, stuck to its piece of wallpaper, he rolled into a tube. He forced himself to get up and concentrate on real life. He stopped a taxi and climbing into the back seat drove off to the airport. 'That's it!' – he decided on the way. Tomorrow a day in Moscow, and then home to San Francisco. *You have to forget childish sentimentality. Some people have lucky childhoods, others don't. There are childhoods that it's better not to return to, neither physically nor in memory. They won't give you anything but constant trauma, suffering from past wretchedness and senseless loss, an inferiority complex, or some mania traumatizing your subsequent life. You should expunge the black past from your own life at least – trash it, liquidate it, forget it.*

Oleg, however, was by no means certain that he could manage to do this. Before getting out of the taxi at the airport he unrolled the wrinkled, yellowed photograph – a last hello from his childhood. The three Nemetses sat on the couch: his mother, radiating youthful, feminine strength, Lyuska being slightly silly and his happy, laughing father. To one side stood the fourth Nemets – a chubby-cheeked boy. He was holding a small violin and bow in his hands, solemnly.